**"I can't believe** ~~school,"~~ he add~~~~~~...~~ **call Dr. Blanton.**

"Not yet," she said, propelling him to the entrance. "I need to talk with Kayleigh."

"She's in her room," he answered, falling into step beside her. "Does this mean you're going to stay?"

Her heart quickened at the hopeful note in his question. She tried not to read too much into it. Going for nonchalance she didn't feel, she said, "Simon says stick close." But it came out sounding flippant, and she saw a cloud darken Max's hopeful expression. Instantly contrite, she tried again, "Yes, I'm going to stay. If you still want me to."

"I put your things in the guest room. Kayleigh is right, you should be more comfortable there."

"Thank you." She ducked her head to hide her smile when he gestured for her to precede him through the door.

*Content Warning: This novel contains discussion of self-harm and suicide attempts as a result of bullying that might prove upsetting to readers sensitive to those subjects.*

# CATCHING A HACKER

## MAGGIE WELLS

**Harlequin**

**INTRIGUE**

If you purchased this book without a cover you should be aware that this book is stolen property. It was reported as "unsold and destroyed" to the publisher, and neither the author nor the publisher has received any payment for this "stripped book."

To the best thing I ever scored online—my Super Cool Party People. From cyber acquaintances to friends IRL, we've been through it all in the last fifteen years. You truly are Top-Tier. My life would suck without you!

**Harlequin®
INTRIGUE™**

ISBN-13: 978-1-335-45723-3

Catching a Hacker

Recycling programs for this product may not exist in your area.

Copyright © 2025 by Margaret Ethridge

All rights reserved. No part of this book may be used or reproduced in any manner whatsoever without written permission.

Without limiting the author's and publisher's exclusive rights, any unauthorized use of this publication to train generative artificial intelligence (AI) technologies is expressly prohibited.

This is a work of fiction. Names, characters, places and incidents are either the product of the author's imagination or are used fictitiously. Any resemblance to actual persons, living or dead, businesses, companies, events or locales is entirely coincidental.

For questions and comments about the quality of this book, please contact us at CustomerService@Harlequin.com.

TM and ® are trademarks of Harlequin Enterprises ULC.

Harlequin Enterprises ULC
22 Adelaide St. West, 41st Floor
Toronto, Ontario M5H 4E3, Canada
www.Harlequin.com

**Printed in Lithuania**

MIX
Paper | Supporting responsible forestry
FSC® C021394

By day, **Maggie Wells** is buried in spreadsheets. At night, she pens tales of intrigue and people tangling up the sheets. She has a weakness for hot heroes and happy endings. She is the product of a charming rogue and a shameless flirt, and you only have to scratch the surface of this mild-mannered married lady to find a naughty streak a mile wide.

## Books by Maggie Wells

### Harlequin Intrigue

#### Arkansas Special Agents: Cyber Crime Division

*Shadowing Her Stalker*
*Catching a Hacker*

#### Arkansas Special Agents

*Ozarks Missing Person*
*Ozarks Double Homicide*
*Ozarks Witness Protection*

#### A Raising the Bar Brief

*An Absence of Motive*
*For the Defense*
*Trial in the Backwoods*

*Foothills Field Search*

Visit the Author Profile page at Harlequin.com.

# CAST OF CHARACTERS

*Emma Parker*—Special agent with the Arkansas State Police Cyber Crime Division. A former troubled teen hacker, Emma is determined to protect kids from the kind of cyberbullying she endured as a teen.

*Max Hughes*—Widowed when his daughter was an infant, Max has dedicated the last seventeen years of his life to his daughter. Now, when her bright future is being threatened, he is depending on Special Agent Emma Parker to make things right.

*Kayleigh Hughes*—A straight-A student, homecoming queen and Ivy League–bound senior at Capitol Academy, Kayleigh is accused of posting hateful things on social media and suspended just weeks shy of graduation.

*Amy Birch*—Capitol Academy's information technology teacher, and the woman Max Hughes dated briefly after meeting on a dating app the previous summer.

*Dr. Samuel Blanton*—Principal of Capitol Academy. A quiet, serious man who has built Capitol Academy into the premier private high school in the state.

*Special Agent in Charge Simon Taylor*—Section chief for the Cyber Crime Division, and Max Hughes's former college roommate.

# Chapter One

"Parker?"

Captain Simon Taylor hadn't shouted her name, but Emma Parker jumped at the sound. She'd been wholly engrossed in studying the data from a series of transactions involving a small florist shop in Eureka Springs, Arkansas. Given the quantity and amounts involved, it was easy to see whoever was sending and receiving the payments was involved in more than simply pushing posies of peonies.

"Sir," she replied, tipping her screen down and hoping the angle was acute enough that her boss wouldn't see what she was studying.

She'd used a backdoor Trojan to bust into the accounts they located. And while it wasn't technically illegal to deploy the silent tracking software when she had cause, it was sometimes hard to make prosecutors believe the information gleaned from legit hacking was on the up-and-up. Her boss hated having to defend their methods to the prosecuting attorney's office. She was hoping to come up with evidence of money laundering so irrefutable, no one would pay much attention to how it had been obtained.

Emma had to blink a few times before her section chief came fully into focus. Though Captain Taylor was under six feet tall, he was powerfully built for a computer jockey. But his physique wasn't what made him impressive. It was the superprocessor he called a brain.

"I need to pull you away," he said without apology or explanation. He inclined his head toward the monitor she'd been glued to for hours. "You recording the data transfer activity?"

"Yeah—" Second-guessing herself, she turned to look at the screen again. A green light flashed in the top right corner. "Yes, sir."

"Come with me."

He turned and headed toward his windowless office. The Cyber Crime Division of the Arkansas State Police was one of the newer sections created by the Department of Public Safety, and therefore not the most prestigious of postings. But she loved it. And though Emma and her colleagues had all gone through the same training and patrol curriculum as their fellow troopers, they were often looked at askance by the other investigators. Most of their work was done at desks, rather than in the field. She and her colleagues spoke a different language. They looked for different types of clues. Ones rarely visible to the untrained eye. But her eyes were highly trained, and damn good.

Emma swiped a hand over the front of her blouse as she rose. She'd dribbled broccoli-cheddar soup down her front after becoming distracted while eating lunch. She had no doubt the dark trousers she had on were creased from sitting too long, even though she'd purposefully bought the kind purported to be "wrinkle-free." At least her shoes were shiny, she thought, glancing down at the new lug-soled loafers she'd acquired over the weekend.

She rounded the corner then drew up short at her boss's open door. There were people in there. A man with dark hair shot through with silver, and a long-limbed young woman with loose waves of hair pulled over one shoulder and downcast eyes. Emma paused in the doorway, her hand braced on the frame. Her chest tightened as she took in the sight of the three of them sucking down all the oxygen in the room.

"Sir?"

"This is Max Hughes and his daughter, Kayleigh," Simon said, nodding to his guests. "Come in and shut the door, would you?"

Emma took a step to her left, then swung the office door closed, trapping the four of them in the cramped office. She put her back against the wall and forced herself to breathe evenly as she scanned the room, desperate to spot an air vent. Simon started talking, but she was having a hard time hearing him over the rush of blood in her ears. Panic clawed its way up her throat. She tried to catch what her boss was saying, but it was—oh, thank goodness. She exhaled long and loud when she spotted the vent placed high in the wall above her head.

"Agent Parker?" Simon prodded. "You with us?"

"Sir. I mean, y-yes, sir," she stammered. Reassured, she forced herself to play catch-up. Gaze traveling over the people in the guest chairs, she did a quick assessment.

The man was wearing quality clothes. Conservative in style. Nice shoes. Freshly barbered hair. He was clean-shaven and the hand he held clasped in his lap had clipped nails, not bitten. *Manicured?* she wondered. Emma fought the urge to curl her own fingers, with their raggedy cuticles and uneven nails, into her palms as she shifted her attention to the daughter.

"...senior at Capitol Academy. Straight-A honor roll, homecoming queen, chair of the community involvement committee and Harvard-bound this fall," Simon said.

Emma took in Kayleigh Hughes's designer joggers and the cropped-but-still-oversize sweatshirt the girl had on, with white-on-white designer sneakers too pristine to have been out of their box for long. A leather bucket bag in a metallic mint green sat at the girl's feet.

As if she could feel Emma's inspection, Kayleigh looked up. Eyes fringed with what had to be lash extensions were puffy and red. If she started the day with any makeup on, it was long gone. Her lips were chapped and cracked. She'd clearly been biting the bottom one. Emma could see a patch of tender pink where the skin had been peeled away.

"...has been sent home for allegedly bullying another girl in her class."

Emma blinked, her head jerking back. "Bullying?"

She frowned as she studied Kayleigh again, slotting this new information into place and seeing how it skewed the data she'd already taken in. Emma knew all about bullying. She'd been a victim of it herself long ago. And being a victim had driven her into retaliation and self-harm, and ultimately into the career she loved.

Sliding her hands behind her back to keep from clenching them into fists, she asked, "What kind of bullying?"

"Social-media posts, mostly," Simon said, nodding in her direction. "The school is looking into the matter, but Mr. Hughes and I go back a long time. He's asked us to look into these posts—"

"Posts Kayleigh didn't make," her father quickly interjected.

Kayleigh started to cry. Were they tears of guilt or fear? Was she upset she'd been caught, or did the girl feel genuine sadness? The need to know the truth gripped Emma like a vise. And she wasn't going to get to the truth through intermediaries.

Dropping to one knee, Emma watched the startled girl's eyes widen in shock as she reared back. "What happened?"

"Trice—" she began, then broke off on a sob. "I would never— We were friends...you know, when we were kids..." She fanned her face and Emma could practically feel her pulling herself together enough to get the words out. "We don't hang much anymore, but I'd never... Trice was so sweet."

Startled by Kayleigh's use of the past tense, Emma lifted her head and swiveled a look between Simon and the girl's father. "Trice...?"

"Patrice Marsh," Max Hughes answered, reaching for his daughter's hand to comfort her. "She and Kayleigh have been friends from elementary school on."

"And what happened to Trice?" She turned to look at Simon.

"She took some pills. Her mother found her in time and took her to the ER. She's expected to make a full recovery," he said, his voice gentling on the last part.

Emma cocked her head, realizing she'd missed something in the introduction. Simon knew these people. This girl. And he called her in here to...what? Prove this girl, who obviously was at the top of the social heap, hadn't picked on someone less fortunate than her? Clearly, Simon didn't have much experience in the world of teenage girls.

"Patrice tried to hurt herself?" She directed the question to Kayleigh.

"Yes, ma'am," Kayleigh mumbled between soft hiccups.

"*Did* you post mean things about her on social media?" she asked directly.

Kayleigh looked up, her gray eyes wide and guileless. "No, ma'am. I swear. Someone must have hacked my accounts. I'd never. Trice and I...we're friends."

"Still?" Emma persisted. When the girl hesitated, she nodded. "You're friend-*ly*, but you don't really hang anymore. Am I right?"

Kayleigh nodded emphatically. "Yes, ma'am. She tried too hard. And could be a bit cringe, you know? But it isn't like she's a total outcast."

"I get it. You don't run in the same circles," Emma concluded.

"No, ma'am."

"And there were posts made by your account about..." Emma paused, unsure if she should use Patrice Marsh's nickname or not. Doing so felt overfamiliar, but on the other hand, she was trying to make Kayleigh comfortable talking about her friend. In the end, she tiptoed around the girl's name. "I take it they were unflattering posts."

"I'd never say those things about Trice. Or anyone," Kayleigh insisted, her bloodshot gray eyes flashing with indignation. "I'm not a bully. I'm not a mean girl, no matter what some people say." She spat out the last few words hotly.

"People are saying you're a mean girl?" Emma asked, holding eye contact.

In her peripheral vision, she saw Kayleigh's father shift in his seat, but resisted the temptation to check him. If he wanted to jump in, he would. She needed to establish a rapport with Kayleigh. Let her know Emma was truly listening to what she had to say.

Kayleigh's chin wobbled, and she drew her poor, abused bottom lip between her teeth. Emma wanted to reach out. Touch her arm. Assure her she hadn't stepped into some empty no-man's-land filled with disapproving adults and Waspish peers, but she had to maintain professional boundaries. So rather than comfort, she offered Kayleigh the consolation prize—attention.

"Can you show me the posts?" she asked gently.

The teen shook her head mutely, then shot a glare in her father's direction. Emma read between the lines.

"You have her phone?" she asked, turning her attention to the thundercloud of a man seated beside his daughter.

He stared back at her with eyes the color of polished pewter and a fierce scowl. "Not because I believe she did anything wrong, but because—"

"Because I told him it was possible her device was compromised," Simon Taylor said, breaking in, his tone stiff and a tad defensive.

She glanced up at Simon, surprised. A straight shooter with a no-nonsense manner, her boss was a cop through and through. Giving people the benefit of the doubt didn't come naturally for him.

She extended her hand. "May I?"

Max Hughes hesitated, but on Simon's nod, he dug into the inside breast pocket of his suit coat. "I saw them earlier," he explained. "Dr. Blanton, the principal at Capitol Academy, had printouts of some posts made on FrenzSpace and PicturSpam accounts with Kayleigh's name and photo, but when I asked Kay to pull up her accounts, they weren't there."

Emma nodded as she took the latest, greatest smartphone from the man's hand and turned it over to his daughter to unlock the home screen. The device was equipped with facial recognition and sprang to life the moment the teenager raised it to her eye level.

"Do you have a code, too?" she asked Kayleigh in a quiet voice.

"Yes, ma'am."

"Does anyone else know your code? Your best friend, maybe?"

Kayleigh shook her head. "No. Not on this phone. I changed it when we set it up."

Interesting. Emma eyeballed the array of app icons on the screen. "Is there a reason you changed it?"

She tried to come off as nonchalant as possible. Emma knew firsthand how quickly a kid could clam up if they thought they were violating the rules of "us versus them." She needed Kayleigh to count her on the side of "us" if she was going to be of any help to her.

"I, uh…" She hesitated, a pale pink flush adding extra color to what Emma could only assume was a spring-break tan. "The old one was from a song I liked, but you know, it was kind of…done. I wanted something fresh."

Emma scrolled from screen to screen. "Were the posts only on those two apps? Nothing on ChitChat or Blabber?"

The question earned her a mild eye roll. "No one uses Blabber anymore. And ChitChat? Really? I'm not, like, thirty," she said, the words dripping with disdain. "Truthfully, I hardly use any of them anymore. I check FrenzSpace sometimes because all the student groups and stuff are on there, but mainly I post pics."

"To PicturSpam?" Emma prompted.

"Yeah." She cast a glance under lowered lashes at her father, then added, "And Foto."

Emma glanced over as Max Hughes's dark eyebrows slammed together. "Foto? What's Foto?"

He directed the question to her, and not his daughter—almost as if he couldn't bear hearing one more surprise from the girl. "It's another photo-sharing platform. More...artistic than social media."

Stormy gray eyes bore into her. "Please tell me *artistic* is not a euphemism."

"I'm not using it as one," she assured him. "But the platform is a favorite of artists, photographers, models and the like." She turned her attention back to Kayleigh. "You posted some photos there?"

After a moment of hesitation, she nodded. "Nothing to get all worked up about. They were some shots Tia and I took at the park. I thought they turned out pretty cool and wanted to, you know..."

She trailed off with a one-shoulder shrug and Emma silently filled in the blanks. Kayleigh was looking for attention—possibly to make contact with someone who knew something about models or modeling agencies. After what had been said about her being Harvard-bound in the fall, taking a detour into the world of clothing designers and cosmetics companies was likely not a part of the plan. But rather than wading into the tangled quagmire of hopes and dreams versus expectations,

Emma carefully steered the conversation back to social media and Kayleigh's posting habits.

She tapped on the icon for PicturSpam and held up the phone to capture the girl's face. Before Kayleigh could get a glimpse at the notifications piling up on her profile, Emma took it back and began to check her most recent posts. She flicked through the last twenty or so without finding anything mentioning Patrice Marsh or vaguely resembling bullying.

"Mr. Hughes, did the principal give you screenshots of the posts the school said came from Kayleigh's account?" she asked without slowing her scroll.

"I have them," Simon announced. "You said PicturSpam?"

"Yes, sir," she replied, glancing up at her boss as he thrust two printed pages at her. "Thank you."

She frowned as she took in the image attached to the post in question. It was the same as on the account she'd pulled up on Kayleigh's phone. But the message tagged @SweetTrice by name, accusing the girl of trying too hard to fit in, and mocking what sounded to Emma like normal teenage foibles and fashion choices. On a scale of mean to cruel, Emma would have clocked it on the less offensive side, but she was no longer an insecure seventeen-year-old. She didn't have a tight grip on what passed for bullying these days, but she could see how the critiques could be hurtful. Particularly when coming from a girl who was once a friend and now sat at or near the top of the high-school social strata.

"You didn't post this." Emma looked up and met Kayleigh's anxious eyes.

"You believe me," Kayleigh whispered. Then her gray eyes filled. Tears trembled on the edge of her lashes, threatening to spill, but not quite making the fall. Yet.

"I believe there are lots of ways to manipulate social media," Emma said, tearing her gaze away to check the other posts on the printed pages. The profile picture was the same.

She squinted at the handle associated with the account. It took her a full minute to pick out the difference between the authentic accounting and the copycat. The copycat had mimicked the original by changing the *i* in *Kayleigh* to an exclamation point. "See? 'At-kayleigh-hughes-oh-eight' on yours, but this one is 'at-kayleigh-hughes-oh-eight,' with an exclamation point in the middle."

Without looking up to see if the girl's lash extensions were being subjected to another flood of tears, she closed the app. "You said the others were on FrenzSpace?"

"Yeah," Simon responded, thrusting the remainder of the papers at her. "Same kind of stuff."

She switched to the app, with its globally recognized navy blue icon, and turned the screen in Kayleigh's direction. She felt the telltale vibration signaling a successful log-in, and tapped until she was in Kayleigh's timeline. The only posts she'd made on the account appeared to be automatically cross-posted from her PicturSpam account. Photo after photo of teens alternately grinning or pouting for the camera filled the page. Though the content was blatantly self-indulgent not one of the captions could be considered cruel.

"You're positive you haven't shared your log-in information with anyone?" she asked, meeting the girl's gaze directly. "No one? Not even your, uh, bestie?"

She was rewarded with a soft snort of derision. "No, I don't share passwords with my *bestie*," she replied, placing excess emphasis on the last word. "We took all the classes, you know." With a glance in her father's direction, she continued, "I know how the internet works. I got an A in Information Technology."

"Don't get snippy, I'm not the one who almost got expelled today," her father reminded her gruffly.

Kayleigh's face crumpled, and in what Emma could only describe as an act of desperation, she reached out and placed a calming hand on the young woman's knee.

"Hey. Listen. I need to look into this more, but I think you've been hacked." She glanced over her shoulder at her boss. "Hacked, or possibly spoofed." Shifting her focus to Kayleigh's father, she said, "If you don't mind, I'd like to hang on to this. I want to monitor the accounts to see if anything pops once word of the day's events gets around."

He nodded his assent. "Oh, it's getting around," he said gravely.

For the first time since Emma entered the room, Kayleigh Hughes sat up straight in the chair. "What? You want my phone?" She whirled to look at her father. "You can't give her my phone."

"I can and I did," he answered calmly. "You'll survive without it for one night."

"But I—" She gaped at her father, practically trembling with teenage indignation. "I have to tell my friends I didn't do it. I need to tell them I didn't make those posts."

"If they're your friends, they'll know you didn't," he countered evenly.

Emma rocked back to sit on her heels. The last thing she wanted was to get caught in the middle of a daddy-daughter spat, so she redirected. "Do you have any other devices linked to this one? A tablet? Laptop?"

Father and daughter nodded. "Both," Max answered.

"I'd like to take a look at them, too, if you don't mind," she said, directing the request to him.

"I can get them and bring them in this evening," he offered.

Emma considered for a moment, then turned to her boss, hoping he was following the same train of thought she was riding.

"Best to see them on the home network," Simon said gruffly.

He had indeed read her mind. Smiling, Emma inclined her head. She shouldn't have been surprised to know they were in sync. The Cyber Crime Division was small, and they'd worked in teams of various combinations over the years. And all of those teams had one common denominator—Simon Taylor.

Max inhaled deeply and stretched his arms up. He let them fall—one to his side, the other landing solidly on his daughter's shoulder. But rather than flinching away, as Emma thought she might, Kayleigh leaned into his touch.

"It's been a long day, and I think we're both ready for some quiet time."

"How about I monitor your phone this evening, then bring it by your house tomorrow," Emma suggested. "I can take a look at the other devices then, but I strongly caution you not to use them." She turned her attention to the father. "I assume you have an office set up at home?"

"I do," he replied, inclining his head. He turned to his daughter. "You can make a couple calls from my computer. Audio only, no video. And no social media."

"But Da—"

He cut her off with a swift shake of his head. "You can tell your friends you're okay, but then we're both going to unplug for the night."

One perfectly groomed eyebrow rose. "Both of us?" Kayleigh challenged. "How will your clients know when to draw breath?"

The teenager's tone was heavy on the sass, but the underlying current of hopeful wonder was unmistakable.

He shrugged. "I guess they'll have to hope their autonomic systems remain functional for the night."

He pulled another phone from another pocket in his immaculately tailored coat and presented it to Emma with a flourish.

"Whoa," Kayleigh breathed. "What if the house catches on fire or something?"

A laugh escaped Emma as she placed the sleek devices on the corner of Simon's desk and rose to a standing position.

A wicked gleam lit Max Hughes's dark eyes as he stood,

too. "If you're really worried, I'm pretty sure I have an old flip phone stashed in the junk drawer."

"Oh, no. I'd rather the house burned down with us in it," Kayleigh replied, and it was tough to tell whether her horrified expression was an act or not.

"Don't say such things," he admonished.

Emma assumed he likely was running on autopilot. She remembered being a teenage girl all too vividly. There was no doubt in her mind Kayleigh Hughes's parents had seen their fair share of hormonal hysterics.

"How should I contact you in the morning?" Emma asked as they gathered their belongings and prepared to leave.

"You can come by. Let's say nine o'clock?" he suggested.

"Sounds good. And Simon has your address?"

"He does. He also has my email if there's an issue." He gestured to his own mobile phone. "I don't know if there's any kind of test you can run to see if there's anything on my—"

Emma nodded. "I'll run some diagnostics and antivirus checks."

Simon handed over a well-used legal pad and pen.

"Let me get your access codes and I'll need handles and passwords for your socials," she said to Kayleigh. "We'll want to reset everything to make sure you're secure, but for now I'd rather not give any indication we think something may be wrong." She gave the girl a sympathetic grimace. "Please don't say anything about our involvement or being hacked to any of your friends. Until we know what's happening and who's doing this, we need to keep things on the down-low."

Kayleigh nodded. "Thank you for not saying 'on the DL,'" she said solemnly.

Emma grinned in response to the girl's deadpan attitude. "I really wanted to," she confessed. Impulsively, she gave Kayleigh's arm a reassuring squeeze. "It all seems bad today, but it will get better. I promise."

"How do you know?" the girl answered morosely.

"I know, because when I was in school, I had something similar happen to me," Emma said bluntly.

"You did?"

This time, Emma was the solemn one as she nodded. "I did. Except I was on the Patrice end of things."

# Chapter Two

"What do you think she meant when she said the thing about being like Patrice?"

Max started at the softly spoken question. Kayleigh had been sullen and silent, staring out the passenger window since they pulled away from state police headquarters. She refused his offer of drive-through sustenance with a shake of her head and her jaw locked shut. He couldn't help feeling that she somehow blamed him for the events of the day.

Or maybe this was nothing more than his own sense of inadequacy rearing its ugly head.

"I have no idea," he said, wading into the conversational opening with caution. "Maybe she was bullied in school?"

She gave a soft snort, but didn't look over at him. "Can't see it. She seems cool."

Max couldn't help but smile. Sometimes, the immediacy of adolescence struck him like an anvil being dropped by a cartoon coyote. Everything in their world happened in the moment. The future was too amorphous and somehow the past didn't count. To them, people were who they were today, and would never change. His daughter met a bright, confident woman who knew a lot about technology and the mores of the online world, therefore Special Agent Emma Parker was cool and cutting-edge. She'd grown up in the era of tech billionaires. She couldn't imagine a world where the computer kids were the outcasts.

But he remembered it.

"I'm sure she is cool. Simon is cool." The derisive snort she gave was enough to convince him she disagreed with his assessment of his old college roommate. "Okay, maybe *cool* isn't the right word for Simon," he conceded. He pondered alternatives, but the best he could muster was: "He's always been really smart, though. Smartest guy I know."

The observation must have struck a chord with his daughter. As he slowed for a red light, he glanced over and found her staring at him, the look of perpetual disdain she'd been wearing for the last few years was gone. He found himself looking into the open and curious eyes of the girl he'd adored since the moment they placed the squalling pink infant in his arms.

"What?" he asked, caution making him slightly breathless.

"You know I didn't post those things about Trice, don't you, Daddy?" she asked, her voice hoarse with fear.

He answered with his heart. "I know, sugar." He reached across the console and gave her clasped hands a reassuring squeeze. "We'll get this straightened out."

"What about Harvard?" she asked, panic filling her voice. "I'm not going to graduate. I won't be valedictorian."

He sucked in a deep breath and returned his hand to the steering wheel as the light changed and the cars ahead of them began to move. "One thing at a time. Let's go home. Regroup. I'm going to call Todd Marsh and check on Patrice. Make sure he and Dara know we're thinking about them. Then I'll call Dr. Blanton."

With a tentative plan in place, they lapsed into silence for the rest of the drive home.

TRUE TO HIS WORD, Max started making calls the moment Kayleigh trudged off to her room. He closed his study door behind him, pulled up the contact list synced to his computer, and used the audio-only option on his desktop to dial a number he hadn't used since the days of elementary-school slumber parties. He wasn't surprised when his attempt to reach out was shunted off to voicemail. Undeterred, he left a brief, but heartfelt, message.

"Todd, it's Max Hughes. I don't know what to say. I hope you know Kay is wrecked. She swears she didn't post anything about Patrice, and I believe her, man. Our girls..." He choked up, then cleared his throat. "I know they've drifted apart, but you know Kay. You know she'd never want to hurt Trice." *Or want Patrice to hurt herself,* he thought, scrubbing a hand over his face. "Anyway, I know we're probably the last people you and Dara want to talk to, so no need to call back. Please know we love Patrice and if there's anything we can do... Yeah, well... Take care."

He ended the call and exhaled in a gust. He allowed himself the space of five deep breaths before opening his email and messaging accounts. Twenty-three unread emails. But there were only nine texts, so he started there.

The first two were from his assistant, seeking direction on how to handle tasks on client accounts. He shot back quick instructions, though he knew the ever-efficient Leah had likely figured things out on her own. Two were auto texts from political candidates seeking donations, another a reminder for a dental appointment the following week. But he slowed his scroll when he saw the name *Amy Birch* pop up next on the list.

Amy was the Information Technology teacher at Capitol Academy. She was also an attractive woman he'd met through a dating app the previous summer. They'd enjoyed one-and-a-half coffee dates before they realized she taught at the school his daughter attended. Indeed, she'd been slated to have Kayleigh in her class when the fall semester started. He'd called it quits on their second getting-to-know-you session before they'd finished their lattes and croissants.

Still, he'd liked Amy, even if the possibility of them dating was out of the question. And because it was a nonstarter, he never told Kayleigh about his near miss with one of her teachers. The teen years had been bumpy enough for them. Coming out of eleventh grade, Kayleigh had her sights set on Harvard and it seemed like things were finally starting to even out between them. The last thing he wanted to do was alienate his daughter. Again.

Darting a nervous glance at the closed door, he clicked on the messages.

Hi. It's Amy Birch in case you removed my number from your contacts. I heard, and wow. I'm sorry. For both girls, I mean.

I can't believe it. I never would have thought Kayleigh could do that.

Sorry. Are y'all okay?

Let me know if there's anything I can do to help.

He wiggled his mouse, gnawing on his bottom lip as he toyed with the idea of responding. But what would he say? Everyone at school thought his daughter was a bully. A mean girl so ugly on the inside that she'd post vile things about a young woman who'd once been her best friend. What could he possibly say?

He clicked out of the messaging app and started moving briskly through his email inbox, discarding junk and flagging items he could deal with later. He was pondering the tax implications of a client request when a message from Kayleigh popped up in his notifications.

Can we order pizza? I need cheese.

He was trying to decide if giving in to her dinner request could be considered a reward for bad behavior when another email appeared in his inbox...from Emma Parker.

Please ask Kayleigh to refrain from using her devices. Thank you.

He blinked at it twice. Kayleigh was messaging him from her room. From either the tablet or the laptop Emma Parker wanted to check the following day. He hit the reply button and began typing: You can see her messages?

I have her phone. Her devices are all connected.

Max stared at the screen wide-eyed. He thought he'd been clever, buying his child devices with a shared platform. He wanted to avoid the tragedy of lost term papers and be sure he could contact her any number of ways. It never occurred to him it would also make it easier for one person to access everything Kayleigh had. Then he thought about all the confidential financial transactions he handled from his home office and his heart began to hammer, and he began typing again: Do you think my desktop is compromised as well?

Are they networked or synced to Kayleigh's?

Max blew out a breath of relief. And typed a quick No in response.

His desktop at home was linked to his office computer. He glanced at the message Kayleigh had sent about pizza and let out a breath of relief when he realized it had come though the operating system's built-in messaging application.

Another message appeared almost instantaneously: Best to keep Kayleigh offline. Pizza might help take the edge off.

Will do. Off to be the bad guy.

He clicked over to his browser to place an order from their favorite local place. Knowing it would take the better part of an hour for the delivery and feeling resolute, he pushed back from his desk. His first stop was the kitchen. He was probably being overcautious, but after what happened with Patrice, he wasn't about to take any chances. After grabbing a plastic grocery bag from under the sink, he opened the slim cabinet beside the fridge and stared at the small pharmacy they kept there.

He stared at the mostly untouched bottle of prescription painkillers left over from when Kayleigh sprained her ankle during a volleyball match in PE. It sat on the top shelf and taunted him with its easy access. His heart flipped over in his chest. He attacked the shelves like a dad possessed. Every bottle of aspirin, acetaminophen, antihistamines and cough syrup went into the bag. By the time he was through, the only things left were a bottle of chalky pink antacid, an elastic wrap and a box of adhesive bandages.

He stalked back to his study, then opened the small closet and kneeled to unlock the safe where he kept important papers, their passports and a stash of emergency cash. Once the bag was bolted away, he changed the digital combination for good measure and pushed to his feet with a grunt.

Then he strode purposefully to his daughter's room. Hesitating only for a moment, he raised his hand and gave the door a decisive rap. He'd learned many important lessons since becoming a widowed single dad to a two-year-old, but one of the most important had come when he and Kayleigh were a decade into their life as a twosome. Overnight, his easygoing kid had turned into a screeching preteen. He'd learned not to even touch the door handle until he heard her muffled invitation to enter.

"Come in," she called, her voice raspy.

He turned the knob and found his daughter sitting cross-legged in the center of her bed, her tablet open to an ever-moving social-media feed and tears streaming down her puffy face. Rushing into the room, he all but threw himself onto the bed in his haste to get to his child.

"Shh. Shh," he soothed, as a giant sob racked her slender body. She twisted her coltish leg under her and turned to him. "Oh, baby, no," he murmured, kissing the top of her head and holding fast. "It will be okay. We'll figure out what happened, and everything will be okay."

"It won't be," she groaned, looking wretched. "Trice is going to die and they all think it's my fault."

"What? No," he quickly assured her. "Patrice is not going to die. She's going to be fine. They may have sent her home already."

He had no idea if the young woman had been discharged from care, but when he'd spoken to Dr. Blanton earlier, the man seemed to be under the impression she would not be held in the hospital much longer.

Kayleigh peeled her face from his shirt and used the back of her hand to wipe away some of the moisture. "It's not just Trice. Now whoever is doing this is posting about Carter."

She waved her hand at the tablet as if he was failing to keep up. And maybe he was. He had no clue what she was talking about. Carter? Kayleigh had gone to the homecoming dance with a guy named Carter Pierce. A football player. Not a boy he would have pegged as his daughter's type. He drove a jacked-up truck and talked as big a game as he played on the field, but under all the bluster and posturing, he'd seemed like a nice enough kid.

Max pulled back, shooting a worried glance at the tablet before looking into Kayleigh's swollen eyes. "What about Carter?"

"They're all talking about him," she whispered, burrowing into him again. "And me. They're saying I told him to do it."

Reflexively, his hold on his daughter tightened. "Do what, sweetheart?"

"But I didn't," she went on, unhearing. "I didn't, Daddy, I swear. You were with me. I don't even have my phone," she insisted.

He pulled back again to look her in the eyes. "Told Carter to do what, Kayleigh?"

Pressing her lips together, she shook her head in adamant denial, tears streaming down her cheeks.

Desperate to find out what was happening, Max reached for the tablet. The feed kept jumping with new posts, so he scrolled down until he saw the handle @kayle!ghhughes08 tagged in a post with a screen capture.

It featured a photo of Kayleigh and Carter Pierce taken at the homecoming football game. She was wearing the short slip dress they'd argued over for hours before she'd bombarded him with picture after picture of her friends modeling similarly slinky dresses and he'd relented. After all, what did he know about teen fashion?

She had on a giant chrysanthemum wrist corsage. Carter was in his football gear, his helmet tucked under the arm. Max had taken the photo himself and shared it and the dozens of others he'd captured with his daughter to be cropped, primped and preapproved for posting.

The post had been generated by the spoofed account, but unless someone was looking closely, no one would ever realize the minor alteration in Kayleigh's screen name. He squinted at the grayed-out timestamp and saw this photo had been shared mere hours ago. Probably not long after they'd left Dr. Blanton's office.

The caption beneath the picture read:

@Kayle!ghhughes08 Framed! OMG I cannot even. As if I'd say mean things about @SweetTrice. We've been besties since birth and ugh! So messed up. @CarterScoresAgain did this. He thinks he can cancel me so he can be #1. TF???? I earned the V. Bruh needs to suck it up and own Salutatorian or go suck on the tailpipe of his swaggin' wagon. IYKYK Amirite? #PrayersforPatrice #besties4eva

A quick scroll up through the feed made it clear many of the commenters believed Kayleigh was trying to deflect blame for Patrice's suicide attempt onto Carter and accused her of encouraging Carter to do the same.

He was opening his mouth to ask what was going on when the doorbell rang. Kayleigh peeled away from him and flung herself into the pile of pillows mounded on the bed. "I don't wanna see anybody."

"Shh," he said, giving her leg a gentle pat. "I ordered pizza, remember? It's probably the delivery driver."

He crawled off the bed, taking the tablet with him. On his way out, he swung past her desk and unplugged the laptop she used for schoolwork. "Let's do what Agent Parker said and stay offline tonight, okay?"

Kayleigh sniffled loudly, and Max decided he would interpret it as assent.

He dropped the tablet and laptop on the hall table, then hurried to the door as the bell rang again. He checked his watch and was shocked to discover less than thirty minutes had passed since he placed their order. Without his phone, he couldn't check to see if it was the delivery driver ringing his bell. Max frowned, annoyed with himself for feeling so bereft without the device. After flicking open the dead bolt, he pulled open the oversize oak door.

"Sorry, I need to grab my wallet—"

He trailed off when he found Special Agent Emma Parker standing on his doorstep, all petite curves and rumpled clothes. The late-afternoon sunlight caught the auburn in her hair. Straight eyebrows drawn down over dark brown eyes, she gazed back at him, her grave expression incongruous with the freckles sprinkled across her nose.

"Sorry, I don't have your pizza," she said in a low voice.

She wasn't supposed to come to his house until the next day, but here she was. Staring at him like he was a puzzle to be solved. Her scrutiny made him want to fidget like a schoolboy. "I thought we agreed—"

He was about to ask if he'd been confused about their appointment when he saw Simon Taylor coming up the walkway behind her accompanied by another man.

Samuel Blanton.

Max's stomach dropped to his feet as he took in the grave expressions the two men wore. Instinctively, he turned back to Agent Parker. "What's happening?"

"There have been more threats made," she began. "Well, posts," she amended. "Other students are reading and interpreting them as harassment."

"Let me guess—they're about a boy named Carter Pierce?" Max asked, directing the question to Agent Parker and ignoring Taylor and Blanton.

"You've seen the posts," she concluded quietly.

"I went up to collect Kayleigh's tablet and laptop, and found her crying." At last, he looked over her shoulder at the men crowding his threshold. "She didn't make those posts. You could see they were from the other account. Even I could see as much," he insisted.

Simon Taylor took a step closer. "May we come in?"

"No." Instinctively, Max raised both hands to stop them from advancing. "I don't... I can't... Kayleigh is already distraught. We can't talk about this anymore tonight."

"Mr. Hughes... Max, I'm terribly sorry to do this," Dr. Blanton said. "Until recently, Kayleigh has been an exemplary student, but these situations can set off a chain reac—"

Max held up a hand. "Please." He heard the edge of desperation in his voice but couldn't be bothered to mask it. "I understand you have to be proactive, but you know something more than what meets the eye is happening here."

He turned back to Agent Parker, willing her to back him up. "You know something is suspicious about these posts."

Her expression softened and she inclined her head in acknowledgment of his plea. "I understand you and Kayleigh are both upset by the events of the day. We know there are duplicate accounts claiming to be Kayleigh, but unfortunately we don't know for certain Kayleigh isn't the one posting to both accounts."

His gaze flew from Agent Parker to Simon Taylor, one of his oldest friends. A man who'd sent congratulations on Kayleigh's birth and condolences when Jennifer succumbed to the cancer first discovered during her pregnancy. "What are you saying? You think Kayleigh is doing this?"

"We're saying we need to rule her out," Simon replied, his tone unaffected.

Max stared at the man as if he'd never laid eyes on him before. How could he even entertain the notion? He knew what they'd been through. He knew how hard Max had worked at being a good parent. Now he dared to stand on his doorstep and imply he'd failed? How dare he insinuate Max had raised a daughter who bullied and belittled other kids? Couldn't they see what was happening? Didn't they understand it was the real Kayleigh who was being framed, not this mean-spirited imposter?

"We have to take all incidences of bullying seriously. You know this, Max," Dr. Blanton said quietly, but firmly. "We must investigate thoroughly and do our best to mitigate any adverse effect this…situation has had on our student body." He pulled his reading glasses onto the end of his nose and peered at the papers he held in his hand. "Surely you understand. If it were happening with any other student, you would expect me to carry out my due diligence, would you not?"

Before he could respond, a battered hatchback pulled into the driveway, blocking the agents and the principal of Capitol Academy in. Max didn't want to know what was printed on the pages the principal held tight in his hand. He only knew he wanted them gone.

Taking two steps back, he snatched the laptop and tablet he'd confiscated from Kayleigh's room from the hall table.

He thrust them at Agent Parker and his gaze fixed on the older man standing behind her. "There. The police now have every one of Kayleigh's devices in their possession." In his sweater vest and half-moon reading glasses, Dr. Blanton looked like a caricature of a private-school headmaster. Max couldn't help wondering if the resemblance was an accident or a choice. "I only ask you refrain from making any life-altering decisions until the police have had a chance to eliminate my daughter from suspicion."

Samuel Blanton hesitated for a moment, then, glancing at the two agents, gave a slight bow. "Kayleigh will remain suspended indefinitely." He removed the glasses from the end of his nose, folded them and used them to gesture to the electronics Agent Parker held cradled to her chest. "We can discuss her possible return to campus once this matter is resolved."

Max nodded and gestured to the young man carrying a thermal delivery box up the sidewalk. "Now, if you'll excuse me, our dinner is here."

Special Agent Parker and Dr. Blanton turned away, but

Simon hesitated, his gaze locked on Max. Impatient with his old friend's awkward social skills, Max waved him off. "Go. Do your job."

But Simon didn't move as the delivery driver edged past him.

"Hughes?" the young man asked, darting the other man a look as he slid the pizza from the insulated carrier.

"Yes," Max responded. He held up a single finger. "Hang tight. I need to grab my wallet for your tip."

"I've got you," Simon said gruffly. Before Max could wave him off again, he pulled his own wallet from his pocket and thrust some bills at the driver. "Keep the change."

The driver handed Max's pizza over to Simon in exchange. "Thanks, man," he said, snatching up his carrier. "Y'all have a good night."

Simmering, Max snatched his pizza from Simon's hands. "You didn't have to."

"You'll pay me back," his friend replied with a shrug. "I put Emma on this because she's my best," he said in his typically blunt manner. "Not only did she experience something similar when she was young, but she's also the best I have when it comes to tracing the untraceable. Trust me. Trust us. We're going to find out who's doing this."

"Whether it's my kid or not," Max retorted, still prickly and defensive.

Simon held his gaze for a moment, then gave a slow nod. "Whether it's your kid or not." He turned to leave, then called over his shoulder, "Eat. Get some rest. If I know Parker, she'll be back here first thing tomorrow."

Shoulders slumping, Max watched as Agent Emma Parker stowed the electronics in the trunk of a nondescript sedan. Simon slid behind the wheel and Max noticed the car had tags declaring the car to be state property. Agent Parker stood back, waiting for the delivery driver and Dr. Blanton to back out before heading to the passenger door. With her hand on the handle, she looked up and their eyes met and held.

She didn't nod or wave. She offered no encouraging smile or other outward sign of support, but once again, he couldn't help feeling she was on their side. Heartened by the thought and buoyed by the aroma of spicy sauce and herbed cheese, he stepped back and swung the door closed before calling his daughter down to supper. When Kayleigh didn't respond, he left the pizza on the dining table and made his way to her room again.

But when he got to her open doorway, he found the room empty, the rumpled bed with its plethora of pillows in complete disarray. His heart hammering in his throat, his gaze flew to the window, as he thought she may have made a break for it. It was closed, the blinds undisturbed.

"Kay?" he called, his voice trembling with the odd mixture of wariness and weariness he'd grown accustomed to feeling when approaching his only child.

No response.

"Kayleigh," he called more forcefully. Making his way down the hall, he peered into the darkened bathroom and found it empty. Impatience warred with worry as he passed the untouched guest room and headed for the primary suite. "Kayleigh, come on. Your pizza is here."

But when he reached the open doorway, he drew up short.

There, on the king-size bed he and Jennifer had bought when they believed they had decades ahead of them, lay their little girl. Kayleigh was all grown up now, curled into a tiny ball on the side of the bed he barely touched, even after all these years. She looked too young for any of this. Too inno-cent to have her whole future come crashing down during second period. He moved to the side of the bed, then perched cautiously on the edge.

"Kayleigh? Sugar?" he whispered loudly. "Pizza's here."

She didn't move and his thoughts dashed to the bag of over-the-counter medications he'd collected from the kitchen cabinet. Tentatively, he brushed her hair back from her tear-streaked cheek. "Honey? You hungry?"

But his daughter only snuffled and snorted, mumbling something unintelligible as she shied away from his touch, curling tighter into a ball. His heart squeezed as if caught in a giant fist as he rose from the bed. Sleep was probably the best thing for her, anyway, and if she felt more comfortable in his room, she was welcome to it. He pulled the duvet from his side of the bed and wrapped her in its warmth.

"I'll put the pizza in the fridge," he whispered from the doorway. "It'll be there when you're ready."

And so would he, he resolved. No matter how long it took.

# Chapter Three

Rather than going home after Agent Taylor dropped her at headquarters, Emma retreated to her desk. She stared at the mobile phones belonging to Max and Kayleigh Hughes, the printed screenshots the school had used as evidence and the devices the girl's frazzled father had handed over at the house. This whole situation stank.

In her tiny cubicle, she checked to be sure the program she'd started running before Simon Taylor pulled her into the meeting with Dr. Blanton from Capitol Academy had completed. Satisfied, she dropped into her chair with a gusty exhale. The scene at the Hughes house struck too close to home. Once, it had been her parents standing in an open doorway gaping at a man flashing a badge identifying himself as an agent with the Federal Bureau of Investigation.

With Taylor gone, the Cyber Crime Division had cleared out for the day. Emma wondered if she should, too. One of the perks of being on the CCD team was they didn't need to work from their desks all of the time. Like most of the other agents in the department, Emma had better, faster equipment at home than the clunky models requisitioned for the Arkansas State Police. Sure, she had to use the laptop to log in to the state systems, but she'd always been a creative person. She found ways to enhance the tools she'd been issued.

She gazed at the detritus on her desk. A pad of paper with

the odd note or numbers scrawled at convenient angles. She leaned forward to collect the scattered pens and markers she'd used to mark up a printout someone had delivered from the ancient dot-matrix printer in the basement of the building. Two monitors, turned vertically, were squeezed side by side on the modular desktop. There was a dog-eared square of sticky notes on top of her docking station.

The only personal item in the whole setup was a plastic hedgehog figurine she'd scored ordering a kids' meal at lunch one day. Her cubicle mate, Special Agent Wyatt Dawson, said it reminded him of her. She took it as a compliment. Hedgehogs might appear spiny, but for the most part they were peaceful creatures. Like her, they were simply content to mind their business. When she said as much to Dawson, he shook his head and said it was because she made all sorts of weird squeaks and grunts while she worked and got prickly when interrupted.

Reaching for her messenger bag, she shoved the printed pages into the outside pocket, then dropped both the phones in, too. The tablet Max Hughes had thrust at her sprang to life when she flipped it over. She reached for the list of passcodes and started tapping in numbers, assuming that Kayleigh would prove to be as lazy as 99 percent of computer users when it came to security. Sure enough, the teenager used the same combination for both devices.

Shaking her head, she set it aside and opened the laptop. She pressed the power button to boot it, but when the operating system engaged, the desktop appeared without any security clearance at all.

"Aw, come on now," she muttered under her breath.

"Someone making it too easy for you?"

She jumped, startled by the gruff question. When she turned and saw Wyatt Dawson leaning an elbow against the partition wall, Emma heaved an exasperated sigh. "Yes. For me and everyone else in the world," she said, spinning her chair to face him. "I'm telling you, people never think about getting some kind of antivirus until it's too late."

"And then only during cold-and-flu season," he replied with a smirk. "You're hanging out late."

She raised both eyebrows. Emma hadn't seen Special Agent Dawson putting in a lot of after-hours time since Cara Beckett, America's favorite lifestyle guru, had moved back to Arkansas. "It appears you are, too."

Wyatt didn't bother to hide his smug smile as he moved into the space next to hers and started gathering his belongings. "Not for long." He slammed his laptop closed, grabbed a couple of files and shoved them all into his bag. "Hear you have a new case."

"Yep. Cyberbullying. Some kids at Capitol Academy."

He let out a low whistle of appreciation. "You're in with the big-time players," he commented. "The blue web has it on good authority the boss hand-picked you for this assignment."

The blue web was what she and her fellow CCD officers liked to call good old-fashioned cop gossip. She rolled her eyes. "You mean the kids of the big-time players," she said dryly. "And you know there's nothing more fun than watching teenagers goad one another into self-destructing."

Wyatt sobered as he straightened. "Right. Sorry." He flashed a wan smile. "We've been poking around in so many dark corners lately, I've forgotten how to be a human being."

She returned his smile with a weary one of her own. "Nah. I know how it is." Glancing back at Kayleigh Hughes's unguarded computer, she decided she'd do well to take the whole lot home with her. Sitting on her comfy couch in her cozy apartment would make slogging through hundreds of hateful adolescent social-media posts slightly less...daunting. Maybe she'd treat herself to a pizza for dinner. The one Max Hughes had delivered to his house had made her mouth water, it smelled so good.

Decision made, she closed the laptop and shoved it into her bag along with the tablet. "Hold up. I'll walk out with you."

Wyatt waited patiently as she gathered everything she needed, then motioned for her to lead the way through the warren of cubicles between their tiny island and the exit.

"Sounds like the boss knows these people personally?" he ventured as they pushed through the double doors into the warm spring evening.

"Looks like it." She shrugged as they crossed to the parking lot. "You know Taylor. He didn't offer up much in the way of backstory."

"I'm sure he didn't. One of the guys near his office thinks he heard something about college mentioned," Wyatt offered as they reached her car. "Can you even imagine Taylor being eighteen and shotgunning beers in some dank basement?"

"Uh, no, I didn't think I could, but thanks for planting the visual," she said, clicking the fob to unlock the doors.

He raised one hand in farewell as he started walking away. "Don't stay up all night creeping on the socials. It rots your brain."

"I'm hoping my translation app has a teen-to-adult setting."

Waving goodbye, she opened the rear door of her car and scanned the interior before putting her electronics-laden bag on the rear seat. She slid into the driver's seat as the lights on Wyatt's SUV flashed. After punching the button to start the engine, she gripped the steering wheel with both hands, then drew what felt like her first full, deep breath of the afternoon.

When she joined Cyber Crime, she knew she'd be called in on cases involving teenagers. She'd hoped to be of more help when it came to sniffing out internet entrapment or thwarting catfishing schemes targeting underage girls. But she wasn't naive enough to think she'd escape without having to confront at least a few cyberbullies. Adolescents armed with keyboards could be some of the most vicious creatures on earth. She knew as much from first-hand experience.

She drove to her midtown apartment on autopilot, her thoughts pingponging between Kayleigh Hughes's predicament and her own past. Her gut instinct was to believe the girl, but Emma knew better than most how duplicitous teenagers could be when they deemed it necessary.

She parked in the designated spot for the condominium she rented in one of Little Rock's mixed use residential-shopping-dining complexes. Her unit was two flights up from one of the many sandwich shops occupying space on the ground floor. With the heavy computer bag digging into her shoulder, she pulled open the door to the shop and was hit with the scent of fresh baked bread.

"Hey, Tom," she called over the chime of the electronic bell.

"Hey, Emma," he answered. "The usual?"

"Yes, please. Extra—"

"Mayo, no tomato, no lettuce," he finished for her. "Gotcha."

She waited near the register while he built her triple-decker club sandwich, selecting a bag of chips and a large cookie in a paper sleeve from the temptations on hand.

"You need a drink?" the man behind the counter asked as he expertly wrapped her dinner.

"Nah, I'm good," she said, presenting him with her second buy-ten-get-one punch card of the month. "Everything going okay here?"

He rang her up, punched her card and bagged her purchases with the brisk economy of movement that robotics specialists dreamed of replicating. "'S'all good. You know, same old, same old."

She waved her debit card at the reader and took the bag from him, waving off his offer of a receipt. "Same old, same old," she echoed. "The way we like it." Turning to the door, she called, "'Night!"

"See you tomorrow," he answered.

Twenty minutes later, she had her sandwich wrapper spread on the antique trunk she used for a coffee table, a cold can of soda and her favorite true-crime series queued up to stream. She took a huge bite of her sandwich, pressed Play on the remote and started pulling devices from her bag as she chewed.

She pulled the laptop from her bag and opened it before setting it aside on the cushion. The tablet was easier to navigate one-handed. Sandwich in hand, she sank into the cushions, half-heartedly listening to the recap of the previous episode as she paged through screen after screen of apps.

Sure enough, Kayleigh Hughes's legitimate account had been tagged in dozens of outraged posts on PicturSpam. She scrolled back a few days in an attempt to pinpoint the moment when the tide of public opinion turned on the homecoming queen and found no hint of the animosity currently running rampant across multiple platforms. Patrice Marsh's attempt to take her own life seemed to have acted as a sort of starter's pistol. In prior posts, the worst she could find was a semifawning comment made by a girl with the handle @DarbyDaBarbie. Kayleigh had posted a picture in which she and two other girls mugged shamelessly for the camera, numbered bibs from a ten-kilometer race pinned to their layered tank tops.

Next to a thumbnail photo of a willowy beauty with long, golden blond waves drawn over one shoulder, DarbyDaBarbie had posted: OMG. Could you stahhhhhp with the awesomeness, @kayleighhughes08? We're getting dewy tryin' to keep up, grrrrl!

Emma clicked open Darby's profile, confirmed the girl was every bit as flawless as the object of her admiration, then checked the timestamp. She'd commented on the postrace photo around ten o'clock the previous evening. There wasn't another mention of Kayleigh Hughes in particular until sometime after lunch.

@CapMarkMorgan2026: Wow. Sad to hear about @SweetTrice. I hope her parents press charges. I swear, girls like @kayleighhughes08 think they can get away with murder.

Beneath his comment others chimed in.

@DooodIKR1113: Or not quite murder. Hang tough @CarterScoresAgain ! #PrayersforPatrice #TeamCarter

@StacezSpam: So. Sad. #PrayersforPatrice And now she's trying to set @CarterScoresAgain up to take the fall?!?! I hope @kayleighhughes08 gets what's coming to her, but you know her daddy is Mr. $$$

@LindC: You mean her zaddy, rite? Whew! Sry, but srsly. Daddy Hugebucks is fire!

And down the rabbit hole Emma went. She scrolled through all the tagged posts on Kayleigh's account, then read through what seemed like hundreds more she accessed through Patrice's PicturSpam handle and various hashtag searches. When she checked Carter Pierce's account, she found the pile-on happening in full force.

And almost no one was attempting to raise a defense on Kayleigh's behalf. It looked like the girl had gone from one of Capitol Academy's most popular and admired students to sea-witch-level villain in less than a day.

Looking up, she realized she'd completely lost the thread on the episode she started, so she decided to opt out. But when she leaned forward to hit the power button on the remote, the screen on Kayleigh Hughes's laptop sprang to life.

Assuming she'd done something to activate the touchpad when she moved, Emma didn't think much about it as she scooped up the other half of her sandwich and switched off the television.

But as her teeth sank into the soft bread, she saw the tiny arrow of the cursor skate across the computer screen.

Frowning, she placed the sandwich carefully back on its wrapper, wiped her fingers on the crumpled paper napkin tucked under her leg and turned to look directly at the laptop. She stared at it, unblinking, not daring to move a muscle in case her hunch turned out to be true. She was about to shake off her suspicions when the tiny green light indicating power to the computer's camera came on.

Acting on instinct, Emma shoved the lid of the device open wide, pointing the camera up at the plain white ceiling. Then she held her breath for what felt like an hour. If the camera was on, the microphone was likely activated as well. Her gaze darted from the green light to the cursor, then back again. Max Hughes said his computer was not linked to his daughter's via a network, but it appeared someone was operating the device remotely.

The hacker?

Gritting her teeth in an exaggerated grimace, Emma slowly slid off the edge of her sofa, trying her hardest not to jostle the computer or make any noise. One knee touched the ground, then she braced her hands on the top of the trunk to transfer the rest of her weight from the cushion. She slipped silently to the floor and was reaching for her phone to record a video, when the cursor skated across the screen and the green light blinked out.

Emma counted backward from ten before exhaling in a whoosh.

She slammed the lid of the laptop closed, then pushed to her feet, pacing the small living room as her mind raced with possibilities.

Did whoever cloned Kayleigh's accounts have access to her computer?

It looked like it.

Were they watching Kayleigh through her camera? Recording her?

Emma gnawed her bottom lip as she pondered all the possibilities.

Where did she keep her computer? Did she carry it with her? No. She likely did everything through her phone. The laptop would have been for homework. Did it stay in her bedroom? Was it always open? Could some creep have been watching her?

Anything was possible, she thought with a shudder.

She'd need to go over all her concerns with Kayleigh's father. The minute she got into their house the next morning, she was going to ask Kayleigh to set up her laptop exactly where it would have been.

Lowering herself gingerly to the edge of the cushion she'd abandoned, she closed her eyes and allowed herself to think like the hacker she once was.

"Backdoor Trojan," she murmured, jumping to her feet again. "But how did they get in? File transfer?"

Knowing she thought better when she was in motion, she rubbed her hands together as she stared hard at the sleek computer. She was about 90 percent sure it hadn't awakened in the time she was scrolling PicturSpam, but she couldn't be certain. She'd need to find out if Kayleigh used any cloud services, or transferred data using portable drives. She hoped Kayleigh was smart enough not to allow Bluetooth connections to drop files onto her devices, but given the lack of security measures in place on any of them, Emma couldn't rule out the possibility.

She fired off an email.

Does Kayleigh keep her laptop in her bedroom?

She stalked the living room, tapping the edge of her phone against her thigh as she waited for a reply. Determining the extent to which Kayleigh Hughes's devices were compromised was not the difficult part. Tracking down MAC or IP addresses would not be difficult, either, though Emma assumed whoever was doing this was also clever enough to use public or communal computers, and was likely good enough to put some misdirection in place. But Emma was good, too. Better than good. She could get through whatever roadblocks their perpetrator threw up. The question was, could she do it in time to stop Kayleigh's life from being derailed and other teens from suffering any additional harm?

She glanced at her phone. No response from Max Hughes.

Her mind racing, she wrapped the remains of her dinner and placed the leftovers in the fridge to take for lunch the following day, then wiped down her already clean kitchen countertops.

Still no reply.

After checking her phone again, she stuffed a load of laundry into the unit's tiny washing machine, then returned to the living room to collect all the other devices. She set up shop at the breakfast bar that separated the kitchen from the living area. A power strip loaded with charging cables kept the juices flowing to Kayleigh's phone and tablet.

She carried Max Hughes's phone over to the small desk, where she had a desktop unit with enough speed and power to run circles around the combined forces of every computer in the Cyber Crime Division, and began running diagnostics on his phone. After checking the operating system for flaws and noting the history and condition of the phone's battery, she ran through the downloaded apps, looking for spyware or other vulnerabilities.

The phone was as clean as could be expected. He didn't

seem to keep any extraneous apps hanging around and didn't appear to have social media downloaded to the device at all. The number of emails hanging out unsorted in his inbox made her left eyelid twitch, but she knew not everyone was capable of striving for inbox zero. She tweaked a few settings to help improve performance and generally button things up a bit, made notes of the changes so she could let him know what had been done, then set aside his device.

The moment she started running the same tests on Kayleigh's notifications, warnings and alerts began popping up like fireworks. She groaned and rocked back in her task chair, lacing her fingers together to keep from starting in on them before the program had a chance to finish processing.

She picked up the tablet, then tapped on the FrenzSpace icon and waited for Kayleigh's timeline to load. The notification icon showed almost two hundred awaiting attention. The built-in messaging application showed thirty-seven private conversation threads.

She didn't want to open one for fear of sending the correspondent a notice their message had been read, but the idea of private messaging stuck. Emma was curious to see whether Kayleigh's friends might be showing their support in a less public forum.

Opting out of FrenzSpace, where required usernames did not allow for much anonymity, she scrolled until she spotted the icon to open ChitChat. The instant-messaging app was one younger generations preferred because they believed it left no virtual footprint. But they were wrong.

People liked it because they could "arm" a Chit with a time bomb, which would make the message disappear after a specified time limit. Character limits within the application ensured messages were short, but not necessarily sweet. Several of her fellow CCD agents agreed that there were few online arenas as brutal as ChitChat. Worse, they thought they could get away with saying anything and everything thanks to the company's highly touted anticapture software, which made getting clear screenshots of messages next to impossible.

For the average user, that was.

But Emma had always been above average when it came to finding work arounds. She'd figured out a staggeringly low-tech answer to ChitChat's so-called security scrambling while consulting on an extortion case the previous year. She might not be able to keep the message from disappearing when time expired, but she would get what she needed. Grabbing her own phone, she opened the camera app.

After capturing a dozen more incoming messages, she closed the application. She studied a half-dozen photos of messages popping up on Kayleigh's feed before she caught a glimpse of the words *kill yourself* in one of them. Though her breath came in a ragged shudder, Emma forced herself to remain calm as she enlarged the photo of the tablet.

Her fingers trembled as she zoomed in on the next. And the next. The last one she read came from a user with the handle @8675309: Girls like Kayleigh Hughes don't off themselves, but maybe someone will do the job for us.

Someone responded with What a waste, and attached a grainy photo of a young woman clad only in a skimpy bra-and-pantie set.

Emma didn't have to zoom in any further to know it was a photo of Kayleigh Hughes. Most likely a still shot captured by the camera on her own computer. One she likely kept open and on, unaware she might be broadcasting her bedroom for all the world to see. Or, at the very least, for this one creeper to see.

Stomach turning inside out, she switched to her email app. Still no response from Max Hughes. Her stomach sank like a stone when she realized she couldn't call to tell him what she suspected. She had his phone.

Clicking over to the case notes she'd typed up after their

initial meeting, she scowled at the blank space where a home phone number would be listed. At the time, she didn't think much of it. People were giving up their landlines. But those people hadn't handed over every mobile device they owned to the police. And now, innocent or not, a young woman was receiving death threats.

She opened an email and pounded out a quick message.

I'm coming over.

A second later, a faint buzzing from Max Hughes's phone confirmed the warning had gone through. Gathering both their phones, the tablet and Kayleigh's laptop, she shoved them all into her messenger bag with her clunky state-issued computer and took off.

## Chapter Four

Max was dozing on the sofa in his family room when his door-bell rang for the second time that night. Swinging his legs to the floor, he looked down at his feet. He'd ditched his shoes long ago, but he hadn't gone back into his room to change out of his work clothes. Pushing off the couch with a groan, he tugged at the waistband of his suit pants and rolled his shoulders. The starched white shirt he'd pulled from his closet that morning was now a rumpled mess. He'd rolled the sleeves onto his forearms before extricating a single slice of pizza from the box earlier, and now the cuffs were accordioned in the crooks of his elbows.

The bell rang again, and he traded his concerns about his appearance for whatever fresh torment awaited him on his porch. He tried to remember the last time someone other than a delivery driver had approached his front door and failed. He missed his phone, and the handy app that allowed him to interact with whoever darkened his doorstep without having to appear face-to-face.

"Coming," he called when it pealed a third time.

Crossing the foyer, he felt a telltale spot of smooth cool tile on the ball of his foot and cringed. Time to buy new socks. He closed his eyes for a moment, gathering himself before tipping his head to look through the narrow strip of glass alongside the huge front door. His visitor was a female. One of Kayleigh's friends?

He flipped on the outdoor sconces and golden light illuminated the porch.

But the woman at his door was not one of Kayleigh's friends. It was Agent Emma Parker. She stood and stared at his door, shifting her weight from foot to foot, practically levitating with energy despite the bulging bag she carried.

He twisted the locks, then yanked the heavy door open wide. "What is it? What's wrong?"

"Is Kayleigh okay?" she demanded, matching the urgency in his tone.

"Yes. Why? What's happening?" He stepped back and gestured for her to enter.

"She hasn't been online, has she?" she asked as she brushed past him.

"No. How would she? You have all of her devices," he pointed out, closing the door behind the agitated agent. "What's going on?"

She blew out a breath, ruffling her hair. "Does Kayleigh keep her laptop in her room?"

He frowned. "Yeah. But you have it," he reminded her, waving a hand at her straining messenger bag.

She reached for the strap of her bag, grimacing as she lifted it off her shoulder and over her head. "Can you ask Kayleigh to show me where she keeps it when she's not carrying it with her?"

He blinked. "Uh, she's sleeping." A thump from the other end of the house made their heads turn in unison. "Or not," he muttered.

"She hasn't been in your office?"

He ran a hand over his face, hoping to brush off the lingering dregs of his own exhaustion.

"I'm not sure. I don't think so. I dozed off." He hooked a

thumb over his shoulder to indicate he'd been in the opposite end of the house. "She was sleeping when I went in to watch TV." She nodded, but the worried crease between her eyebrows didn't go away. "What's the matter?"

The dull thud of a drawer or door shut with a tad too much force prefaced a disembodied, but clearly annoyed, voice that called, "Da-a-a-ad?"

"She's definitely up now," Agent Parker murmured dryly. "Why do I feel the urge to step in front of you?"

"Part of me wishes you would," he said in a low voice. "But don't worry, I'm used to being the villain around here."

Emma took a small step back as Kayleigh stormed past them, her sights clearly set on the family room and his office beyond. She drew up short in the hall, scenting her quarry and doubling back, her angry gaze fixed on him. "Did you take my computer?"

The parent in him cringed, embarrassed by her rudeness, but he didn't have the energy to open a second battle line in their ongoing power struggle. "I did. We're both staying offline, remember?"

"What did you do with it?" Kayleigh demanded.

"I gave it to Special Agent Parker." He gestured to the woman watching them go back and forth like a couple of tennis players fighting it out on center court. "You remember Special Agent Parker?" he prompted, unable to keep the snarky edge from his voice. "The police officer looking into your alleged hacking."

The moment the words were out of his mouth he wished he could suck them back. If Emma Parker didn't latch on to the underlying tone, Kayleigh certainly would.

He wasn't wrong.

Both women zeroed in on him.

"Alleged?" Agent Parker asked. "You have reason to believe your daughter's devices were not compromised?"

"I knew you didn't believe me," Kayleigh accused. "You never believe me anymore."

Max took a step back, raising his hands in surrender and shaking his head. "I didn't mean it to sound like I didn't believe you."

"How did you mean it?" Emma asked, surprising both him and his daughter with how quickly she leaped to Kayleigh's defense.

"I'm tired and...stupid," he said, giving up on mounting a stronger argument. "I say stupid things when I'm tired. Everyone does."

Without another word, Agent Parker turned to face Kayleigh head-on. "Y'all can call me Emma. I have your laptop, phone and tablet." She darted a glance in his direction. "I came because I also have your father's phone, and it occurred to me you might not have another way to call for help if needed."

"You think we might need help?" Max asked.

"I think there's a lot going on, and neither of you needs to feel isolated," she replied. Emma pulled his phone from her bag, and handed it over to him. "I checked it. Yours is clean."

"Can I have mine back, too?" Kayleigh asked.

Emma shook her head. "I'm afraid not. I have reason to believe your phone has been spoofed, meaning all the applications you use on both your phone and your tablet are likely breached. I also believe your laptop has been ratted."

"Ratted?" Kayleigh repeated. "What's that?"

"I mean someone has installed a kind of spyware. It allows them to access your computer remotely. RAT stands for Remote Access Trojan. Like the wooden horse from Greek mythology, a program sneaks into your operating system by looking like a normal file. Once it's in, it unleashes all sorts of nasty code. Depending on what's written into them, they can tie up or delete files, slow your operating system, infect programs, monitor your online activity, access stored data, clock your keystrokes and basically control the whole thing."

"Someone has been sneaking into her computer?" Max asked, aghast.

"I think so. I noticed some suspicious activity earlier, but I had to shut it down. I didn't want whoever was controlling the device to know someone was onto them." She turned to Kayleigh. "Would you show me where you usually keep it?"

Mutely, the teen nodded and turned on her heel. Max fell into step behind them, his mind racing. Infected files? Spyware? Suspicious activity?

"What kind of suspicious activity?"

Emma shot him a pointed look over her shoulder. He figured he was supposed to know what her glare meant, but he was as clueless as he'd been when Dr. Blanton had called him and asked him to come down to the school. Was it really the same day? Time was both whizzing past and moving at a snail's pace. Deciding the smarter thing to do was to follow her lead, he zipped his lips and stuck close.

"Do you power your laptop down at night?" Emma asked as she stepped into Kayleigh's room.

"No, ma'am," his daughter replied.

"Do you close it, or put it in sleep mode?"

Kayleigh shook her head. "I usually just plug it in. I mean, it goes to sleep after a while, you know."

"I know," Emma confirmed. Pulling the computer from her bag, she handed it to Kayleigh. "Don't open it yet. Set it down in the spot where you usually keep it."

"O-kay."

A tiny furrow appeared between Kayleigh's eyebrows. Max figured there had to be a wrinkle as deep as the Mariana Trench between his. He watched as Kayleigh placed the computer on the desk. His gut twisted as he pictured the laptop open, the light from the screen saver acting as an unofficial night-light for a girl who was too old to admit she wanted one.

"Do you recall noticing any times when your computer woke without you touching it?" Emma asked Kayleigh.

His daughter frowned in concentration, then shrugged. "I guess so. I figured they come on every once in a while, you know, to let you know it has power."

Nodding absently, Emma moved to the desk. She stood in front of the computer and turned in a slow semicircle, her gaze skimming over the dresser, the bed and the door leading to the en suite bath and walk-in closet.

Max stood frozen in the doorway, torn between wondering what she was thinking and fear that he knew where this was heading.

"I assume you video-chat on here sometimes?" she asked, gripping the back of the desk chair.

"I did when I took a remote class or we had to meet for group projects," Kayleigh said, then shook her head dismissively. "But most of the time I use my phone."

"Is it safe to say you don't use your laptop as much as your phone or tablet?" Emma asked, her tone neutral and business-like.

"Yeah, definitely."

Emma opened the laptop, then stepped to the side as she plugged in the power cord. Reaching across the trackpad, she wiped and tapped until a program for the built-in webcam opened and a wide-angle view of his daughter's bedroom filled the screen. Apparently satisfied with what she saw, she clicked out of the program, then gestured for them to leave the room.

The three of them stepped into the hall, but when Max glanced back, he saw she'd left the computer sitting open on the desk. "Are you going to—"

Emma pointed in the direction of the main part of the house. "Let's go in here to talk."

She lifted her bag and strode down the hall, leaving them no choice but to follow. Once in the living room, the heavy satchel hit the floor with a soft *thunk* as she sat on the ottoman situated in front of the sectional sofa, gesturing for them to take seats across from her.

Max smirked, vaguely amused to be shepherded around in his own home. He was used to issuing the orders. He should have been annoyed by her overreach, but he didn't have the energy to work up his outrage. Besides, he couldn't help but admire her confidence. She was clearly in her element.

"I think someone is controlling Kayleigh's computer remotely. Most likely they gained access through what we call a backdoor Trojan. Like I told you earlier, it's a type of spyware that rides in attached to a file or program."

Kayleigh turned to her father, instantly defensive. "I haven't been downloading random apps. I swear."

Emma shook her head hard. Max reached over to place a calming hand on Kayleigh's arm. "It's okay. Let's hear what Agent…Emma has to say."

"It doesn't have to come from a download. If you use any kind of cloud service or share files with other students, a memory stick you might use to save work in the school computer lab, an email. There are all sorts of ways someone can get in." She waved a hand as if to clear the air. "The how isn't as important as the who and what." She leaned in, bracing her elbows on her knees. "My job is to figure out who it is, and what they are doing."

She paused for a moment, then looked Kayleigh in the eye, treating her like an adult. An equal.

"The thing is, for me to figure them out, I need to be as sneaky as they are. And I'm going to need your help."

"My help?" his daughter asked, shooting a worried glance in his direction. "I don't know anything about this stuff. I mean, I took an IT class, but only because it was required.

I've never been too into computer stuff, you know, beyond social media."

"You don't have to worry about the technical side of things. Tech is my job. All I need you to do is be you," she said, reaching into the bag at her feet. "Now, I'm going to show you something and it may be upsetting," she warned. Then, slipping a glance at him, she added, "To both of you."

Max turned to look at his daughter, but she was nodding.

"Okay," Kayleigh said eagerly.

"No, honey, hang on—" he began.

"Daddy, I have to," she said, cutting off his protest at the knees. "No one believes I'm not doing this stuff. You don't even believe me—"

"I do—"

"Allegedly." His baby, the girl he'd dedicated his whole existence to for nearly eighteen years, pursed her lips and arched an eyebrow at him like he was a worm squished on the pavement. She'd drawled the word he'd carelessly used minutes earlier.

Max felt the last of his defenses stripped away. She was right. This was her life they were talking about. And in less than two months, she'd be eighteen and flying the nest. If they could get her through graduation. Turning his attention to Emma Parker, he nodded his acquiescence.

"Do what you need to do."

"Someone posted this on ChitChat earlier tonight."

She pulled her phone from the bag and pulled up a picture. Max grimaced and turned away as soon as he recognized the girl in the grainy screen capture. Someone had posted a photo of his daughter in her underwear. His heart thudded slowly in his chest. Was this really happening?

"How did they…?" Kayleigh cut herself off. "Ew, is that my bedroom?"

"Looks like it to me," Emma confirmed. "I suspect whoever is behind this has been using your webcam to capture footage of you in your room. This has all the signatures of a still grabbed from a video stream."

"You said you got it off ChitChat?" To his surprise, Kayleigh took the phone and squinted at the image. "How? I thought Chits couldn't be screen-capped?"

"Their encryption makes it hard to grab them, but sometimes the easiest way around advanced technology is to go old school." She took the phone back from Kayleigh. "I pulled the app up on your tablet, then took a picture of the screen. Not the best resolution, but I grabbed a bunch before they disappeared."

She flashed an impish smile Max found oddly reassuring. This wasn't just a determined woman, but a clever one. Emma Parker had the will to find a way.

Now he understood why his old friend Simon assigned this agent to the case rather than taking it on himself. Simon was a by-the-book guy. The quintessential linear thinker. He didn't color outside the lines or think outside the box. Max had no doubt Emma Parker would kick her way out of any box she encountered.

"So smart," Kayleigh whispered on an exhale. "I'm totally doing that."

"Anyway," Emma said, shaking off her moment of tech triumph. "I don't want to tip whoever is doing this off, so I want to set the computer up in your room again."

Max saw Kayleigh's eyes widen and opened his mouth to protest, but before he could get a word out, Emma held up a hand. "No, I'm not suggesting you let this creeper go on watching you."

"Then what are you suggesting?" Max asked.

"I think we need to role-play the removal of the computer," she said slowly, as if letting the idea unfurl. "We need to make it look as normal as we can, because we don't know when our watcher will be watching. But first, I need to get more information, so I need to let them pop in a few more times."

"But I can't...ew. You want me to let him watch me sleep?" Kayleigh protested.

Emma pulled a face and Max realized she was holding back from telling them this creep had likely been watching her for some time.

"Obviously, you shouldn't undress or even sleep in there, but I'd like to set it up so we can track it. Once we get what we need, we can make it look like you and your dad got in a fight over being suspended, and he takes it away. The trick will be playing it out when we know they are looking."

"How will we know?" Kayleigh asked.

"We wait for the computer to wake. If it does, we watch for the light indicating the webcam is in use. It'll be our cue."

"I'm supposed to sit there and watch it?"

Emma shook her head. "Nope. Again, the tech is my job."

"You're going to what? Camp out in my room?"

Max caught himself staring at Emma Parker with the same incredulity his daughter voiced. Would she? Sit there all day and all night, waiting for this predator to show themself?

"I don't know if this will work. All I know is I don't want you in there."

"But won't you be all weirded out, knowing someone might be watching?" Kayleigh asked, concern in her tone.

"I plan to stay out of camera range. After we get what we need, I can cue you guys and all you have to do is...fight."

"Well, we can certainly fight," Max said dryly. "But we don't know when or if they will, uh, pop up. It could be days."

"I have a feeling they're going to want to look in fairly often now things are happening," Emma said with a sympathetic wince. "I mean, wouldn't you?"

Max couldn't contain the guffaw. He couldn't imagine purposefully wreaking such havoc in an innocent stranger's life. "I suppose, if I were some kind of cyber stalker," he conceded.

"Listen, I didn't really think all this through until I was on my way over here, but I think it's a good plan." She turned to Kayleigh. "If I get tired, I'll sleep in your bed. My hair is dark enough to pass for brown in low lighting. If I keep the covers pulled up, they'd see nothing more than a lump in the bed, anyway."

She tossed off another one of those shrugs, and Max couldn't help but wonder what drove Special Agent Emma Parker. He couldn't recall meeting any woman so obviously unconcerned with her own comfort or needs. Did she even have a toothbrush with her? Did he have a spare in the house?

"I can do my work from anywhere," Emma explained, gesturing to her bag. Turning to him, she said, "Call Simon Taylor. Ask him if he thinks this is a good idea. If he tells me to stand down, I'll leave."

"Don't leave," Kayleigh interjected, surging to the edge of the sofa cushion as if to intercept the agent. Then his daughter turned to look at him. "I think we need to try."

Max shifted his jaw as he thought the agent's impulsive plan through. He knew he'd give in, but he needed a moment to process it all. If this was what Kayleigh needed to feel safe, he'd do it. If this unconventional approach to investigating this incursion into their privacy was what it took to get his daughter's life back on track, of course he'd do it.

But inviting a strange woman to sleep in his home? In his daughter's bed? He wasn't sure he was impulsive or unconventional enough to agree to this plan.

Zeroing in on the earnest agent seated across from him, he asked, "You don't mind if I call Simon and run this past him?"

Emma's smile was slow, but certain. "Not at all. As a matter of fact, I'll call him myself."

As she tapped the screen to place the call, Max knew it

would be a moot point. She placed the call on speaker. Simon answered on the second ring.

"Taylor."

"Chief? I'm here at the Hughes house with Max and Kayleigh, and we want to run something past you," she said in a rush.

"Go ahead," Simon prompted.

"What would you think if I were to stay here and set up a sort of cyber stakeout?"

# Chapter Five

Emma awoke in a strange bed the next morning. She blinked at the pale aqua wall blankly, then groaned as consciousness seeped in. She was in Kayleigh Hughes's room. She'd camped out in there, setting up her surveillance in accordance with the plan she and Simon Taylor concocted on the fly. Max and Kayleigh hadn't appeared to be convinced, but they'd provided her with fresh sheets, a slice of pizza and an unopened travel toothbrush bearing the name of a local dental practice.

She'd worked late into the night, as was her habit, relying on the glow from her own laptop and the ceiling fixture in Kayleigh's preposterously large walk-in closet to light the room. Her plan was to stick to the shadows or under the covers, providing enough movement to satisfy whoever was controlling Kayleigh's webcam.

Emma had seen the camera activate twice before she'd become too sleepy to sit propped against the wall. Satisfied her tracking software was running, she'd brushed her teeth in the adjoining bathroom, then crawled into Kayleigh's bed.

Snuggled into the warmth of the covers, she took in her surroundings. The room was the perfect aqua-and-white backdrop for a girl on the precipice of adulthood. There were dozens of photos tucked into a beribboned memory board above her desk and strings of white fairy lights draped from the crown molding.

Emma squinted at the bright sunlight streaming in around the edges of the blinds and wondered if Kayleigh Hughes would ever feel bright and beautiful in this room again. Her privacy had been breached. Her reputation was shredded. And her perception of what her peers thought about her, well, there'd be no putting the genie back in the bottle.

The soft whir of her laptop fan caught her attention. She peered over the edge of the bed in time to see the screen flash to life. Seconds later, Kayleigh's did, too.

"Oh," Emma gasped, pulling the sheet up high enough to cover most of her head, then rolling off the edge of the bed onto the floor.

Had the watcher peeked in while she'd been sleeping? After the sun came up? Had they noticed her red hair?

Emma was lying flat on the floor, her neck twisted so she had a direct view of her screen.

The cursor moved.

She smiled her satisfaction. She'd successfully cloned the clone. Her desktop was now a perfect replica of Kayleigh's... at least on the surface. Now all she had to do was wait to see what their stalker's next move would be.

The waiting was the absolute worst part of her job.

She watched as the cursor moved to the icon for a video-conferencing application popular among teens, postpandemic. Emma was torn between derision and admiration. It was such an obvious place to spy from, and yet, beautifully effective. Almost everyone Kayleigh's age used the application at one time or another. How better to hide in plain sight?

The cursor zipped across the screen to the camera control panel and Emma peered at her screen as the bedroom view filled the screen. Thankfully, the angle was good. She was completely hidden from view on the floor, but had she not bailed from the bed when she had, the slash of sunlight cutting through the blinds and hitting the pillow would have given her away for sure.

She was taking in the view, wondering how long they'd dare to stay connected, when a knock on the door almost jolted a yelp out of her.

Emma clamped her lips shut, then glared at the screen. If she spoke, the person watching may realize she wasn't Kayleigh. She closed her eyes, willing whoever was on the other side of the door to go away without speaking.

No such luck.

"You up?" Max Hughes called through the door.

Thankfully, he hadn't called her by her name. "Don't say my name. Don't say my name," she whispered into the fluffy white chenille bedside rug.

"Uh, there's breakfast if you want it," he said, raising his voice a few decibels.

"Go away. Go away," she muttered.

"Okay, well…" She squeezed her eyes shut, willing him to walk away. "Okay," he said in gruff defeat.

She turned her head. In the sliver of space between the bed skirt and the polished floor, she saw a shadow move past. She exhaled into the preternaturally clean space under the bed. What kind of teenager didn't keep stuff squirreled away under her bed? She puzzled for a moment, then turned her attention back to the computer.

Her screen was back to its replica of Kayleigh's wallpaper. A crimson block letter *H* on a snow-white background.

Harvard.

Kayleigh was planning to go to Harvard in the fall. She was a student leader with perfect grades and a list of extra-curriculars like a rap sheet. Homecoming queen.

Did she even have time to wreak havoc on her fellow students? Why would she? Some kind of revenge? She was almost done with high school. The finish line was in sight. Soon they would scatter to their fancy colleges, pledge fraternities and sororities, and move on to law school or med school, or corner offices in Daddy's investment firm. What could someone like Kayleigh hope to gain from tearing down the kids around her? She already had it all in hand.

Wriggling around, Emma pushed up enough to rock back onto her heels.

She looked down at the short shorts she'd borrowed the night before. Her shorter, curvier body pushed the seams of the clothes she had no doubt were fashionably slouchy on Kayleigh's long, lithe teen frame. Glancing over at the navy pants and rumpled, stained white shirt she'd discarded on a chair, she winced. She decided to worry about her wardrobe later and marched into the bathroom.

After splashing water on her face and brushing her teeth, Emma availed herself of one of Kayleigh's hair bands, pulling her hair into a ponytail as she wandered into the massive closet. In the back, buried behind a selection of winter-to-spring coats and jackets, she found exactly what she needed— a long, thick terrycloth robe.

Shrugging into it, she hummed her appreciation as she belted the sash tightly. She'd dash home, change and pack a couple outfits…just in case.

Following the scents of coffee and bacon, she found her way back to the kitchen. She spotted Max Hughes standing at the island, with his back to her. His hair had been recently barbered. She could see the thin line of paler, newly exposed scalp along his nape. He wore dark jeans so perfectly pressed she had no doubt there was an empty dry cleaner's hanger in his closet. His broad shoulders were perfectly encased in yet another crisp white dress shirt, but the sleeves had been neatly folded back to expose tanned forearms. As he lifted an oversize white coffee mug from the marble island, she hesitated, trying to determine the best way to approach, when she noticed his feet were bare as well.

"Good morning," she said, pitching her voice low, not wanting to startle him.

It was no use. His hand twitched and he yelped as hot coffee spilled down the front of his shirt.

"I'm so sorry," she said, grabbing a striped towel from the counter and rushing to the island. She thrust it at him, stopping shy of mopping the mess from his chest. "I didn't mean to scare you."

She was babbling. Of course, she hadn't meant to surprise him, but she had. The best thing she could do was cease and desist. She froze in place, the towel dangling in the space between them.

"Sorry," she repeated.

"No." He shook his head and took the towel from her. "My fault. I was zoning out."

Flashing a wan smile, she nodded to his streaked shirtfront. "Well, at least you haven't left the house. I usually trash my clothes after I get to work and have to walk around wearing my shame for the rest of the day."

His smile came slowly. "Yeah. Thank goodness for small favors." He gestured to a thermal carafe parked beside a coffee maker that looked like they'd lifted it from a high-end café. "I can offer you plain old drip. If you want something fancier, we'll have to get Kayleigh involved. She doesn't like me messing with the settings," he explained as he tossed the towel onto the counter, then lifted his mug for another attempt.

"Drip is perfect," she assured him.

"Mugs in the upper cabinet."

Emma located another one of the big white mugs and filled it halfway with the rich, dark brew. Lifting it to her nose, she took an appreciative sniff. This was nothing like the scorched sludge they called coffee at headquarters.

"Do you take milk or sweetener?"

Her lips curved into a smile, and she shook her head as she wrapped both hands protectively around the mug. If it tasted half as good as it smelled, she wanted to savor every sip. "No, thank you."

They both raised their mugs. She blew across hers to cool it before hazarding a cautious sip, but he drank deeply. She figured he'd been up awhile.

"I have egg bites," he said, moving around the island to her side.

Her eyebrows rose as he slid open a stainless-steel drawer to reveal muffin-shaped scrambled eggs flecked with what looked like red peppers, cheese and bits of breakfast sausage. Their uneven sizes and crispy cheese edges made them almost look homemade. Then she lowered the mug and took a sniff.

"Did you make these?"

He nodded. "They're not anything fancy. Kayleigh goes back and forth on the whole to-carb-or-not-to-carb question, so I try to go protein-heavy in the mornings."

She lowered her mug, her jaw dropping as she took in his nearly pristine white shirt. "You cook?"

He cocked his head to the side, an amused smirk tugging at his lips. "You think I've been raising my child on a steady diet of chicken nuggets and toaster waffles?"

She gave a helpless laugh. "Maybe?"

He chuckled, too. "I cook. I also clean." She pulled a horrified face and he pressed on. "I also do laundry, but not as often since I accidentally shrank one of Kayleigh's sweaters."

"Yes, well, shrinking sweaters is grounds for termination," she said, matching his sober tone.

Max waved an expansive hand around the kitchen. "I'm not saying I don't have help here and there, but for the most part, I'm fully domesticated."

"I'm both chastened and impressed." Giving him a small

bow, she plucked one of the breakfast muffins from the drawer. Emma immediately regretted her impulsiveness. This wasn't the kind of kitchen made for scarfing a quick bite standing over the sink.

"Here." He picked up the towel she'd thrust at him moments before and handed it off. She took it whispered sheepishly, "Thanks."

Grinning, he spun and pulled a small white plate from the open shelf beside the cooktop. "I can offer you a fork and a seat as well," he said as he held the plate under her breakfast.

She widened her eyes. "A fork? Cutlery would mean I'd have to eat two."

Without another word, he pulled a dinner fork from a drawer, speared a second egg muffin and deposited it on the plate.

Her cheeks flamed, but she didn't wave him off. Scooting around the island, she inclined her head toward one of the stools. "Here?"

"Please."

"Thank you," she murmured, pulling the padded stool out so she could slide onto it.

Thankfully, he turned away to top off his own coffee mug while she got settled. "Did anything happen last night?"

She nodded as she chewed. Chasing the delicious egg concoction with a slug of coffee, she used the dish towel she'd co-opted as a napkin. "Yes. Three hits noted. I'll have to check my software to see if they attempted to peek in while I was asleep."

He turned to face her, his mouth thinned into a tight line. A tiny muscle in his jaw jumped and Emma wanted to kick herself for her insensitivity. She wasn't a cop spouting off the facts for a superior officer. She'd blithely told this man some stranger had likely been sneaking peeks at his daughter while she was blissfully unaware.

"I'm sorry," she said gruffly. "I was… I'm sorry."

He pursed his lips so hard the edges of them turned white, then swallowed hard. "I, uh…" He paused to take a ragged breath. "It's done, right? We know now. We're on to him. Her. Them. Whoever," he said with an impatient wave of his hand. "You should be able to trace it? With your software?"

She nodded. "Yes."

Emma shoveled another bite into her mouth before it could run off without her brain engaged. Pinpointing their culprit would be more complicated than a simple trace, but there was no reason to get too far into the weeds with him.

"Listen, I'm at your disposal," he said, shifting gears abruptly.

Her shock and confusion must have shown on her face. He set his cup down on the counter with a clink and ran his hand through his dark hair, ruffling it out of its neatly combed style.

"I, uh—"

He raised a hand to stifle her stammering. "I mean, I'm taking time off work. I can handle any emergencies from here, but this…" He paused, gulping in a breath and looking around the opulent kitchen as if seeing it for the first time. "Kayleigh is my everything. This…situation has my undivided attention."

"I understand, but the best thing you can do is keep living your life and let us do our thing." She offered him a wan smile as she prodded the second scrambled-egg muffin with the tines of her fork. "We might be a small department, but the CCD is mighty."

"Oh, I know." He opened his hands to show he meant no offense. "Simon is proud."

She smiled. "He handpicked each and every one of us."

"I heard."

"I was going to suggest the two of you get away, but Simon thinks it's better if you stay put."

"Nowhere to go, anyway." He gave his head a slow, sad shake. "It's me and Kayleigh against the world."

"Grandparents?"

"All gone," he said with an almost apologetic shrug.

"Simon said Kayleigh's mom passed when she was young?"

"A week shy of Kayleigh's second birthday," he said, a hint of gravel in his voice. "Jen was twenty-six weeks along when she found a lump. Metastatic breast cancer. She had a lumpectomy at week thirty-two and started chemo as soon as she delivered, but…" He shook his head.

"I'm sorry."

Though the words were heartfelt, they sounded small to Emma's ears. Inadequate. But they were all she had. She stared at the large, capable hands splayed atop the marble island, trying to imagine this quietly controlled man attempting to manage the unmanageable. Cancer. A newborn. Widowerhood. Parenthood.

Setting the fork down, she straightened her shoulders and met his gaze. "I'll catch the person who's doing this."

"I'm counting on it," he said gruffly.

After pushing the plate away, she wrapped her hands around the coffee mug and drew it closer. "I have to tell you, whoever is doing this is almost certainly using public internet access. This is someone who knows what they're doing. This isn't television. We're not going to pinpoint an IP address and find some oblivious loner hanging out at a desktop in their parents' basement."

"Simon already told me the cautionary tales," he assured her.

"We have to be smart. Careful. And at times, it's going to mean moving more slowly than you'd like."

"Understood."

"The moment we tip our hand, they could simply 'poof,'" she said, making an exploding gesture with her fingers. "Slip off into the ether, never to be heard from again."

He raised his open palms. "I can't think of any other way to tell you I get it."

"Cool." She nodded and slid off the stool. "Thank you for breakfast." After taking one last gulp of coffee, she carried her plate, fork and mug to the massive farmhouse sink, but he stepped in to intercept her.

Disconcerted, she began to babble. "I'm running diagnostics on last night's activity now. Once I have what I need backed up to my laptop, I'll run home and change, then go into headquarters. I'll meet with the team and put together a game plan. I hope to be back here by about noon."

His eyebrows rose as he rinsed the dregs of coffee from her mug. "Kayleigh and I don't have to stay in the house, do we?" He grimaced. "I mean, we can go out?"

"I'd advise against going out much. Not only are we dealing with a stalking situation, but Kayleigh is getting some pretty upsetting backlash online."

He stiffened, his movements jerky as he turned off the faucet.

She blew out a soft sigh. "I want to minimize her exposure. We both know what a small town Little Rock can be. I'd hate for someone to spot her out and about and use seeing her to spin a narrative about Kayleigh being unfeeling, given what happened with Patrice Marsh."

"Ri-i-i-ght," he said, drawing out the word.

"We're living in a world made of perception, Mr. Hughes—"

"You slept in my house last night. I think you can call me Max," he interrupted, a sharp edge in his tone.

"And perception is the reason we should do our best to observe propriety, Mr. Hughes."

"Fine, Special Agent Emma Parker," he replied mockingly.

She raised her hands as she backed away. "I'm only trying to make this as easy on you as I can."

"Nothing about this is easy, Special Agent Emma Parker,"

he grumbled. "I'll make sure we place ourselves under house arrest."

Inhaling deeply, Emma counted to three then let his anger roll right off her as she exhaled. "Thank you. Please leave Kayleigh's computer as it is until we have a good bead on our watcher. Remind her to keep an eye out for the green light and assume nothing in her room is private."

"This is a nightmare," he muttered as he slotted the dish and mug into a dishwasher hidden behind a cabinetry panel.

"No, sir," she said softly, but firmly. "This is not the nightmare. I know what's happening to Kayleigh is upsetting, but I can give you a half-dozen ways this could be worse off the top of my head."

"I didn't mean—"

Emma shook her head in dismissal. "This situation is frightening, possibly dangerous and absolutely damaging to your daughter's reputation," she allowed. "But as it stands at this moment, the biggest consequence Kayleigh is facing is the possibility she may not get to attend her first-choice university."

"Now, wait a minute—"

Emma didn't want to hear his attempts at forming a defense. "While such an occurrence would be unfair and possibly a threat to her future, at this time she still has a future. A bright one. Even if Harvard bails on her."

"I'm not—"

She cut him off. "There are photos of your daughter partially dressed out there. Their existence alone could push this case to another level. We need you to be patient. Give us the chance to catch this creep."

He inhaled deeply, but rather than the anger and frustration she braced for, he simply exhaled in a gusty whoosh and dropped his head, nodding his acknowledgment.

"The internet is an amazing place, Mr. Hughes," she said softly. "Things blow up bigger and faster than we ever imagined, but within a day, they are old news. People may dredge something up years from now, but it won't have the same impact as it has in the here and now. Social media is to traditional media what cable news was to the newspaper. Gossip and speculation are the fuel of the online world. Your job is to help Kayleigh keep everything in perspective."

"Right," he said, his voice rough with pent-up frustration.

Emma looked directly into his pewter eyes, smiled and spouted the words her grandmother used to use on her when the world closed in on her. "I promise—this, too, shall pass."

AN HOUR LATER, Emma walked through the doors of the state police headquarters, her laptop bag slapping against her hip. She'd stopped at her apartment long enough to shower and change clothes. Simon Taylor was sitting at her desk chair when she reached her cubicle.

"I hear you told Max Hughes his privilege was showing," he said by way of greeting.

"Not my intention," she replied stiffly.

Simon shrugged. "Eh. It probably was. Max has always had a sort of master-of-the-universe way about him. Even when he didn't have the proverbial pot to use for toilet training."

She slid the computer bag from her shoulder, then placed it on her desk as the section chief rose from her seat.

"I simply reminded him his daughter is a bright, accomplished young woman. Even if Capitol Academy opts to expel her, she won't have any difficulty meeting equivalency requirements and landing a spot at a top-tier school."

"Particularly since her father has deep pockets," Simon said with a brisk nod.

Emma smothered a smile. Simon had a reputation for being abrupt and abrasive. He called things as he saw them and spoke his mind without even attempting to finesse his words.

It was a trait she appreciated in a superior, but knew did not serve him well when it came to a smoothing his career path.

"Did you get any hits?" he asked, pivoting to the task at hand.

"Yes. Unfortunately, each one pinged a different MAC address. Three from fast-food restaurants, one a coffee shop and the last the unsecured router of a small upholstery company on the north side of the river."

"Randomized," he concluded with a frown.

"Yes, sir."

"You're going back for more?" he asked with a curt nod.

"Yes. I'm going to copy my data over for Wyatt to poke at as well," she informed him.

"Copy me, too," he said, pushing away from the cubicle wall. "I assume you're staying there tonight?"

Her head jerked up. It took every ounce of her willpower to fight back the blush threatening to flood her cheeks. Knowing she wouldn't be able to hold it at bay if they got into a discussion about her sleeping arrangements, she latched on to the order he'd issued.

"You want me to copy you as well?"

He gave a soft snort. "Don't act so surprised, Parker. It's not unusual for me to look into cases."

True. In the past, he frequently poked his nose into ongoing investigations. And with his ability to slide into some kind of hyperfocus mode, he often proved to be quite helpful, drilling through mountains of data with laser-like precision. But for the last six months, the boss had become increasingly fixated on the activity surrounding an online smuggling ring they believed to be running out of a small town in the northwest part of the state. It had been a long time since Emma heard him ask for anything more than the most cursory of updates on any other case.

"I'll send it over now..." She turned her head as Wyatt Daw-

son came around the corner, a laptop cradled on his forearm
and his phone clutched in the other hand.

"You sending over your sleepy-time footage?" he asked,
flashing a distracted smile at their boss as he sidled past to
deposit his computer on the desk behind her. "There's a betting pool on whether you drool in your sleep."

Emma rolled her eyes. She didn't doubt there was such a
pool. Cops would bet a couple bucks on just about anything.
"I do not drool."

"Everyone drools," Simon said in his matter-of-fact way.
"It's more a matter of whether your stalker captured the moment or not."

She bit her lip, then turned to face him. "I know *stalker* is
the correct word, but for the sake of the Hugheses' peace of
mind, I've been using *watcher* instead." His eyebrows and he
pinned her with a questioning stare.

"Watcher, huh?" Wyatt repeated, too busy plugging in and
arranging his devices to his liking to even glance up. "You've
invented stalker-lite. Still creepy, less threatening."

She bit her lip, then shrugged. "I'm trying to keep a seventeen-
year-old from completely freaking out."

"Good call," Simon said with a decisive nod. "Forward your
footage and findings. I'd like you to set up a time to speak with
Patrice Marsh's parents, then I need you back on watcher duty."

"Yes, sir," she replied.

"I think it's safe to assume we're looking for someone with
Capitol Academy ties, but I'd like to nail down something
more specific in the next day or so. You know how the cycles
run on these things. If they don't get whatever it is they want
from framing Kayleigh, they'll either push harder or find another kid to pick on."

"They're already testing those waters from what I saw online last night," she said grimly.

"We have to keep moving on this. See if you can get Kayleigh to open up more, get her talking about her friends," he suggested.

She gave a huff of a laugh. "I'll try."

"You can do mani-pedis," Wyatt suggested with a smirk.

Before she could retort, the boss stepped in. "You have good instincts for this stuff, Parker. Go down the rabbit holes. We'll be your backup. You can pass off anything that feels off-kilter to you to us, and the team will do deep dives," he said, hooking a thumb in Wyatt's direction. "I want you nipping at their heels."

"Understood," Emma said with a nod.

"Good." Simon thumped the top of the partition twice, then spun on his heel and marched off, already moving on to the next thing on his list.

"Another slumber party at Richie Rich's house, huh?" Wyatt teased. "Hey, does he have one of those miniature trains you can ride all over the house?"

"Sadly, no," she said, all mock solemnity. "But he did make these really yummy breakfast bites made out of scrambled egg, cheese, diced-up peppers and big hunks of sausage. You should get Cara to make some for you…oh, wait. Your guru girlfriend is vegan, isn't she?" She tipped her head in mock sympathy. "Never mind."

"Not vegan—vegetarian," he corrected, but she could hear the sulk in his tone.

"Oh, well, you can have the eggs, peppers and cheese, I guess," she said with a laugh.

"And the meat-alternative sausage is actually pretty good," he said unconvincingly.

"Keep telling yourself you love it," she cooed. "Now, leave me alone. I need to offload some files to my backup so I'm free to go chase bad guys."

# Chapter Six

When Emma Parker returned to his house, she blew in like a tornado.

A tornado carrying a plastic laundry basket filled with folded clothes, and the straps of two computer bags criss-crossing her chest like bandoliers. A tall, dark-haired agent crossed the threshold on her heels. "This is Wyatt Dawson," she said breathlessly. "He's on our team."

Max smirked and took the man's proffered hand. "We're a team now?"

"I think she means I'm part of the Cyber Crime Division," Wyatt responded genially. "Our Emma is all about getting things done faster. She forgets to connect the dots sometimes."

"Yep. Connect on your own time. I'm setting some stuff up in Kayleigh's room," she said as she pivoted. "Is she in there?"

"She's, uh, no. She's in the media room," Max answered, his attention following the auburn-haired dynamo marching to the hall leading to the bedrooms.

"What's happening?" Max asked the other agent as they followed in her wake.

"We've identified the locations where the, uh, watcher, routed through, but they're all public hot spots. Not uncommon when someone is familiar with masking software. Unfortunately, we can't trace beyond the relay point unless we get in there while they are active in the software," he explained. "So we're setting some more equipment up so we can hardwire in. We don't want to leave a digital footprint our perp might spot."

"Okay." Max wasn't sure he was following the plan entirely, but it sounded like these people were planning to camp out in Kayleigh's room indefinitely. "So this is something you all have to be here for?"

The agent beside him shook his head as they stopped outside Kayleigh's bedroom door. Emma was already in the room, rearranging items around the desk. "I'm going to help Emma set up and test everything."

At last, Emma straightened, using her foot to scoot her laundry basket off to the side. "If they keep up the pattern they showed yesterday, I think we can get a hit on them fairly quickly." She turned and looked at him head-on, her gaze direct, but wary. "Only trouble is, I will need Kayleigh to hang out in here with me."

"You want to use my daughter as bait," he said flatly.

Her eyes flashed and she looked like she wanted to jump down his throat, but when Agent Parker opened her mouth, her tone was calm and reasonable. "No, I want your daughter to carry on living her life exactly as she was the day before yesterday."

"The day before yesterday, I wasn't under house arrest," Kayleigh said, startling them both.

"Kay." Max pressed a hand to his chest as he turned to find his daughter leaning against the wall behind him. "I didn't hear you."

"You're not under house arrest," Emma said, craning her neck to look past him.

"Virtual house arrest," Kayleigh insisted. She stepped around him to peer into her room.

Wyatt Dawson looked up from the computer and smiled when he saw her. "Hey."

"Hi," she replied. Turning her attention to Emma she asked, "What's up?"

"This is Agent Dawson. He works with me."

"I figured as much."

Unfazed by mild sarcasm, Emma Parker continued. "We're setting up to try to catch them watching live so we can pinpoint where they are accessing from. They use masking software. We'll need to have you in here so they have reason to stay online longer."

"Watching me," Kayleigh said, wrinkling her nose. "So creepy."

"I know, right?" Emma replied.

Max watched the byplay between the two of them like a spectator at a tennis match. This total stranger seemed to have an in with his daughter Max hadn't had in years, and watching them together both hurt and heartened him. He wanted Kayleigh to connect with someone, even if it couldn't be him.

"So I sit here staring into space and waiting for the green light?" Kayleigh asked.

"Well, you don't have to stare into space," Emma replied.

"I don't have my phone. I can't get online. What am I supposed to do?" Kayleigh retorted, her tone edging toward combative.

Emma let out a huff, then pulled a book off one of the shelves over the desk and tossed it to his daughter. Kayleigh caught it reflexively, then sneered as she looked down at the cover of a once-beloved teen romance.

"Seriously?"

Emma rolled her eyes, then returned to helping Agent Dawson set up. "Stare into space, for all I care. Pretend you're doing a makeup tutorial. Clean out your sock drawer—"

"Sock drawer would be off camera," Dawson pointed out, nodding to Kayleigh's closet-slash-dressing room.

"Good point." Emma turned back to Kayleigh. "Dance party? Yoga?"

"Or get a jump on studying for your physics final," Max interjected. Everyone in the room stopped and turned to him. "What? Midterms weren't great and you can't coast your way into an Ivy League school. You're suspended, not expelled. You still have to keep up."

Kayleigh stared at him, her expression a mixture of pettiness and disbelief. "Daddy, I'm not going back to school."

"What? Yes, you are. They're going to catch whoever is doing this and—"

"She's probably right, Mr. Hughes," Emma said, looking up from her work. "Even if we clear everything up, the school may not want the disruption. Kayleigh could finish out her senior year remotely."

"But…graduation. You'll be valedictorian," he argued. But the words sounded weak and whiny to his own years. Reality set in like a stone sinking in his stomach. "You won't walk at graduation," he concluded, shoulders slumping.

Kayleigh leaned into him, and a lump rose in his throat. He was the father. He should be consoling her, not the other way around. But now… Taking advantage of the moment, he wrapped his arm around his daughter and pulled her close into his side. "I'm sorry, baby. This is all happening so fast."

"I know."

Her whispered response nearly broke the dam holding back the emotion rising inside him. But there were two strangers in the room, and though they were pretending not to watch, their family drama was playing to an audience. He kissed the top of Kayleigh's head, then loosened his grip before she could wriggle away.

"Okay." Max cleared his throat. "We'll give it a few hours, but we're getting out of the house this evening, even if it's only to go for a bike ride."

The two agents nodded as they worked, and Kayleigh gave a noncommittal hum, but he was banking on restlessness winning out.

"There," Agent Dawson said, rocking back to sit on his heels. "All set."

A laptop running code on a black screen sat beneath the desk, a wire connected it to a dongle attached to Kayleigh's computer. With a few keystrokes and a tap on the trackpad, an exact replica of Kayleigh's desktop appeared on its screen.

Emma nodded and typed in a few commands. A moment later, she nodded. "I'm in, too."

Max shifted uncomfortably from foot to foot. They made it all look so easy. Too easy. "You guys are scaring me with how quickly you can get into all this stuff."

Agent Dawson rose to his feet, slapping his hand across the front of his jeans. "Nah. We do this all the time. Most people wouldn't have a clue, believe me."

Max did believe him because he hadn't had a clue, and he'd always thought he was fairly tech-savvy. The last two days had debunked him of the notion. He hadn't even heard of half the applications Kayleigh and Emma discussed, much less knew what they were for or how to get into them.

The agent looked down at his partner. "You all good here?"

"All good. Thanks for your help." Emma stood as well. "Agent Dawson and rest of the CCD team are going to be helping track down any background information we may need." She turned to Kayleigh. "I'm going to be checking socials on my devices throughout the day. I may need you to clarify some things or identify some of the subjects."

"In between makeup tutorials and sun salutations?" Kayleigh asked, raising her brow to match her mocking tone.

Agent Parker was quick on the uptake. "Exactly. But don't look to me for help with the physics stuff. I lost interest after an apple fell from the tree."

"I guess you could say you're relatively slow," Dawson said, nudging Emma as he walked past.

She groaned in response. "Sheesh, Wyatt. If anyone should be telling the dad jokes around here, it should be him," she said, pointing in Max's direction. "You don't even have kids."

"Oh, don't get him started," Kayleigh groaned. "My dad thinks he's hysterical."

Boggled by how quickly everything circled back to him, Max shook his head. "Hey, wait a minute. How'd I get to be the target here?"

"You're the default dad," Kayleigh said, shooting him a wicked grin.

Max laughed, too happy to see his daughter's smile to care if he was the butt of every joke she ever made. "Lucky me." He turned to Agent Dawson. "Come on, I'll walk you out while these two argue over who gets to braid whose hair first."

"Age before beauty," Emma Parker said as they started down the hall.

"Are you gonna be the braider, or the braidee?" Kayleigh retorted.

He chuckled, shaking his head as he and Wyatt Dawson made their way to the foyer. "Thanks for your help with this."

Wyatt took his hand and gave it a firm shake. "I really am nothing more than backup. Emma's the best with this stuff. If anyone can figure it out, she can." He paused, as if debating whether he should go on. When he spoke, it was clear he was choosing his words with care. "Emma went through some stuff when she was younger than your daughter. She's a good resource, you know, for someone to talk to."

"For Kayleigh or for me?" Max asked.

The younger man shrugged. "Either." He reached for the door to let himself out. "If you need anything more, have Emma give us a shout."

"Will do," Max assured him. "Appreciate your help."

He watched until the other agent slipped into a nondescript SUV. When he pulled away, Max spotted a silver subcompact parked to the side of the semicircle drive. It was a newer model. Shiny in the afternoon sunlight, but otherwise unremarkable. A car built for fuel efficiency and likely purchased for reliability. A vehicle for people who preferred substance over style, he mused as he engaged the locks on his front door.

A no-nonsense car for a no-nonsense woman.

He puzzled over the laundry basket as he wandered back toward Kayleigh's room. Was it possible she didn't own a suitcase? A duffel bag? The more likely explanation was she didn't want to take the time to pack. He smirked, thinking back to his long-ago bachelor days. Once upon a time, he'd thought nothing about dressing out of a hamper. At least the clothes she'd hauled in looked washed and folded.

The murmur of soft feminine voices drifted down the hall. Kayleigh spent hours laughing, chatting, giggling and squealing with her friends in there, but this was different. His steps slowed. He'd never heard Kayleigh speaking to a woman like this. It was conversational. Easy. Low-key. Stripped of the forced brightness or heightened self-awareness of interactions between teenage girls, the timbre of his daughter's voice was richer. Fuller. A smooth, self-assured alto.

She sounded so much like her mother.

The realization struck him like a physical blow. Leaning against the wall outside her room, he pressed the back of his head into the drywall and gazed at the ceiling, trying to recover the breath knocked out of his lungs.

"So what did you do?" Kayleigh asked.

"I didn't deal well," Emma replied.

The vagueness of her answer likely frustrated his daughter as much as it did him, but to her credit, Kayleigh didn't push. He smiled as his bright, inquisitive girl tried a different approach.

"How'd you get over it?" she asked.

"Who says I did?" Emma returned without missing a beat.

"Is what happened to you why you do this?" Kayleigh persisted.

"Absolutely."

Emma's unequivocal answer startled a laugh out of him. The occupants of the room fell silent, and he knew he'd given away his position. But this was his house, and he wasn't about to be made to feel like the interloper here.

Turning so he stood square in the doorway, he asked, "Can I get you anything?"

"I'm fine," Emma replied, looking up from her laptop. "Thanks."

"What are we having for dinner?" Kayleigh asked then.

Max blinked as she unfolded her long, coltish legs, then repositioned herself like she was animatronic origami. "We ate lunch an hour ago."

"Can we go out?" she persisted. "Maybe get Greek salads from Garden of Paradise?"

Max shifted his gaze to Emma, then back again. "Depends on Special Agent Parker."

"As I said before, Mr. Hughes—"

"Her name is Emma, and his is Max," Kayleigh interrupted with a huff. "Sheesh, it's not like she didn't sleep in my bed last night. This Mr. Hughes, Special Agent Parker stuff is sounding...weird, you know?"

He startled when he spotted the cop sitting on the floor. "Agent Parker?"

"Emma is fine," she muttered, returning her gaze to the computer in front of her. "As for going out, can I convince you to give it one more night?" She looked up at Kayleigh, her expression frank. "I know you haven't been online today, but I can tell you it's still not pleasant."

Kayleigh took this in, her nostrils flaring as she pursed her lips. "I didn't do anything wrong. It's not fair—"

Emma held up a hand to stop her. "I know. It's totally not fair, but it is reality. Perception is reality at the moment. Until we can nail down proof, people are going to believe whatever they read."

"Whatever happened to innocent until proven guilty?" Kayleigh cried.

"It's a nice idea, isn't it," Emma returned without missing a beat. "Unfortunately, it's pretty much only true in a courtroom, and sometimes not even there. The person who controls the narrative, controls the court of public opinion."

Max stood in the doorway, watching the two of them go back and forth. For the first time in nearly eighteen years, he was not the person Kayleigh looked to for answers to her questions. It was both a relief and a knife to the gut.

"I think we should listen to, uh, Emma," he said, inserting himself into their stare-down. "One more night. But maybe we can take the bike ride I mentioned earlier?" He turned to Emma. "We have an extra mountain bike if you want to join us."

She raised an inquiring eyebrow. "You keep an extra bike? I thought the toothbrush was impressive."

Kayleigh snorted. "I have a trail bike and a ten-speed. Dad got really into cycling for, like, a minute and a half."

"Or ten years," Max interjected, feeling suddenly outnumbered. "Still am. Not that you'd notice," he added in an undertone.

Emma caught it, though. She cocked her head as she looked up. "Cycling, huh? Do you wear the funny aerodynamic helmet and the shorts with the padding?"

"It's so embarrassing," Kayleigh groaned, flopping back on her bed, her legs still twisted into a shape he couldn't imagine was comfortable, much less sustainable.

"I wear gear appropriate to the sport," he replied stiffly. "When I was in college, I was a track racer."

"Oh, God, this is where he tells you how cool he used to be," Kayleigh said, speaking to the ceiling.

Emma chuckled. "Did you, now?"

"I think I'll head for the other end of the house. Shout if you need anything," he said gruffly.

"Hey, Max?" Emma called after him.

Startled by the sound of his own name, he stopped in his tracks, then turned slowly. "Yes?"

"Once we pinpoint a location, don't forget I'm going to need you and Kayleigh to be ready to do a I'm-taking-your-computer-away-for-your-own-good performance," she said, dropping her voice an octave in what he could only assume was supposed to be an imitation of him.

"I'll practice my lines." He turned on his heel.

"And, Max?" she called again, and he turned back slowly. He replied in an exaggerated drawl. "Yes, Emma?"

"Oh, now you're going to make first names weird," Kayleigh complained to no one in particular.

"I'd love to go for a bike ride later," Emma said, unperturbed by the teen's mockery. "I think we can all use a break."

He nodded. "Sounds good."

"As long as you don't mind if I skip the spandex," she added, a wicked gleam lighting her eyes.

"Yeah, no uniforms required," he conceded, feeling unexpectedly awkward. Shifting his attention to his daughter, he scrambled for more solid footing. "Maybe we'll ride and get Garden of Paradise to-go. We can earn one of those salads."

"There's no such thing as earning a salad, Dad," Kayleigh said, pushing onto her elbows. "You bike for ice cream or cookies, not salad."

"I don't believe food has to be earned," Emma said, turning her attention back to her screen. "It's ridiculous."

"I know, right?" Kayleigh exclaimed, sitting up again. "I mean, who decided salad was good and ice cream bad, anyway?"

Max chortled. "The FDA, maybe?"

"Dad," Kayleigh groaned, shooting him a look he secretly named the Side-eye of Scorn.

"I'm going," he said, lifting his hands in surrender. "But you blew your chance to score both salad and ice cream," he called over his shoulder as he walked away.

He'd gone no more than three steps when he heard Kayleigh pick up the thread of the woman-to-woman conversation he'd interrupted. "I really hate how everyone is so fixated on food. I try not to be, but it's hard when you know girls who tally up everything on their lunch tray, and then I feel like I'm doing something wrong, you know? I mean, if you're going to feel bad about something, why not focus on something with more of an impact, like recycling, or something."

"I hear you," Emma agreed.

Unable to help himself, Max lingered in the hall. Kayleigh was rambling on about all the things teenagers should be doing rather than obsessing over all the things teenagers have obsessed over for decades when his phone buzzed in his pocket. Kayleigh stopped talking midrant, and a strange stillness settled on the house.

He pulled the device from his pocket and saw he had a text message from Emma. It contained only two words.

Green light.

Within seconds, Kayleigh was up and bustling around her room as if she wasn't moving random objects from one spot to another. Almost a full minute passed before he heard the muffled thump of his daughter flinging herself across the bed.

"You can't keep me locked up forever," she shouted into the hall.

Max flinched, even though he knew she was only spouting lines Emma had suggested. He didn't respond. According to Emma, their watcher might get spooked and ditch if they thought he was nearby. It was better to let them think Kayleigh was bored and restless and pushing back against her confinement. Whoever was doing this was determined to disrupt her life. It was better to let them think they were winning.

Pressing flat against the wall, he listened to Kayleigh muttering and grumbling, every nerve in his body tingling with the need to rush in. To protect her. But he couldn't. If they were going to catch this creeper, they had to be every bit as sneaky as the perpetrator.

Kayleigh got up and started stomping across her room, playacting at living her normal life. But everything was upside down. Her voice grew watery, and soon her complaints were being punctuated with sniffles. Max squeezed his eyes shut and clenched his fists as he listened.

It seemed to go on forever.

At one point, he caught himself holding his breath and had to force his lungs to exchange oxygen at something resembling the usual rate.

He checked the time on his phone. Three minutes had passed since Emma sent the text.

Kayleigh managed to keep going, though. He heard something hit the wall at about the five-minute mark, but the thump was soft. Unlike her gasping sob.

"They can't kick me out of Harvard," she called out to no one in particular. "I've already been accepted. They can't take it back," she insisted with all the forceful naivety of someone who still believed life was driven by absolutes.

He wanted to rush in there and grab her. Put an end to this

farce. Three more minutes had passed. Was this reprobate getting their kicks watching a seventeen-year-old girl fall apart?

Max figured it had to be another kid. What would an adult hope to gain from this torment? No, it was probably another student. A clever one, who knew too much about how technology works. He didn't think so at first, but knowing what he did about how Emma honed her skills, he was reassessing.

His phone vibrated.

All clear. Come in.

He rushed into Kayleigh's room and found her crumpled on the bed, her cherished Harvard hoodie balled in a wad beneath her as she cried softly into her pillow.

"Shh, sugar," he whispered, jostling her as he perched on the side of the bed. He reached across to hold her.

Praying she'd turn into him instead of away, he braced himself for rejection. But once again, she curled into him. He pulled her up, banding his arms around her as she heaved a sob. Resting his chin atop her head, he glared at the agent sitting cross-legged on the floor, tapping on her keyboard.

The lid to Kayleigh's laptop was closed. Relieved to know no one could be spying on them, he exhaled in a whoosh. "I hope you got what you needed, because we're not doing that again," he said, his voice rough with emotion.

"It certainly should have been enough," Emma murmured distractedly, her fingers flying across the keys.

He rocked Kayleigh gently, refusing to loosen his grip even when her sobs turned to hiccups. A series of pings reverberated in the quiet room. He could see Emma's phone on the floor beside her. The incoming messages moved at such a clip he wondered if she was even able to get the gist of them.

Then her spine straightened and she pulled her hands

away from the keyboard as if she was afraid to go a key-stroke too far.

Her phone chimed again. This time, she glanced down to check the message.

"Got it," she said briefly.

"Where are they?"

She pursed her lips as she read the message again. "It'll take a bit more time to pinpoint a device, but we can confirm the signal we picked up as routing through the Coffee Cup franchise on the six-hundred block of Capitol Avenue origi-nated three blocks north of there."

"Three blocks north?" He frowned as he tried to envision the coffee shop and its surrounding environment.

"Yes." Emma met his gaze as Kayleigh lifted her head from his shoulder. "Capitol Academy. The posts are coming from inside the school."

## Chapter Seven

By the time Emma finished giving an update to the rest of the team and an impromptu video conference with her boss, she was more than ready for some fresh air. Kayleigh and Max had decamped the minute the calls had begun.

If the offer of a bike ride was no longer on the table, she'd blow off some steam with a jog on the quiet, tree-lined streets that wound down the city side of the high bluffs above the Arkansas River. Rummaging through the basket of clean laundry she'd brought from her condo, she unearthed a pair of running shorts and a clean T-shirt, then ducked into the bathroom.

Toeing off the thick-soled loafers she wore to work, she tried to recall whether the gym bag with her running gear was still in the trunk of her car. The last thing she wanted to do was to ask the teenager she was supposed to be protecting to loan her some sneakers.

She pulled a hair tie from her computer bag, then slid down the empty hall in a pair of no-show running socks. Reaching for the handle of the large front door, she hesitated. The display panel on the wall opposite the entry showed the security system was armed.

"Crud," she muttered, letting her hand fall.

She'd hoped to slip out and check to see if she had shoes before letting the Hugheses know she was ready to escape.

Biting her lip, she eyed the display, wondering if she could disarm it without a code.

"Hey."

She let out a startled yelp, pressing her hand to her chest to calm her jumpy heart. "Hi," she said, cringing at her reaction as she turned to find Max watching her from the kitchen doorway. "I was, uh—" She hooked a thumb over her shoulder. "I need to go to my car."

"Oh." He moved to the alarm panel and jabbed in a series of numbers. Three beeps signaled the all clear. "There you go."

Glancing self-consciously down at the toes of her socks, she nodded. "Thanks. Left one of my bags out there."

The moment he stepped aside, she yanked on the door handle and escaped. Thankfully, her gym bag was still in her trunk. She also spotted a small bag containing skin-care samples she'd scored when one of the women in the department had an in-home party sponsored by a cosmetics company. She'd forgotten it was there. Unzipping the gym bag, she exhaled a breath of relief when she spotted her battered running shoes nestled inside. She also pulled out the sleeve she wore to hold her phone while she worked out. Back when she worked out, she amended, slipping it onto her forearm so she wouldn't forget it. Sitting on the bumper of her car, she wriggled each foot into the shoes.

Emma was trying to force air into her compressed lungs when a pair of pristine men's athletic shoes entered her field of vision. She twisted her own laces around her fingers to keep from jerking upright.

"You still up for a bike ride?" Max asked.

"Sure," she said, trying to keep her tone casual. "Unless you and Kayleigh would like to go on your own."

He chuckled. "I think at this point, Kayleigh would pay you to go along."

"I'm already being paid," she said as she straightened,

planting her hands on her hips. "I'm here to do my job," she said, using a smile to soften the reminder.

"And we appreciate it." Unfazed, he hooked a thumb over his shoulder. "I got the extra bike down and we got it cleaned up. We can grab dinner while we're out."

She bit her lip. "Probably best to call something in. I think we should shield Kayleigh as much as possible. When we get there, I can go in and pick it up."

"Sounds like a plan."

He hovered nearby as she pulled the bags from her trunk. When she turned, Emma was gratified to see him looking as uncomfortable as she felt.

"We do appreciate what you're doing, Emma," he said, using her first name with deliberate care.

"Like I said, I'm only doing my job," she insisted.

"I'm not a fool. If it weren't for my relationship with Simon, I wouldn't have a trained agent staying in my house because my daughter got into some kerfuffle on the internet." He gave her a wry smile. "We both know this goes above and beyond, and I'm aware of our privilege."

"But you're not afraid to wield it," she said, the words popping out before she could stop them.

"No," he admitted, a self-deprecating smile tugging his mouth down. "Not when it comes to protecting my daughter. I'll do anything to make sure she's safe."

"You'll do anything to make sure she's cleared," she corrected. "You didn't go to Simon because you thought somebody was threatening Kayleigh. You went to Simon because you thought Kayleigh was threatening somebody else, and it would reflect badly on her."

She watched the color creep up his neck and stain his cheeks, but he didn't look away. "True. Initially," he insisted. "But things have changed."

Emma inclined her head. "Things have changed." She

slammed the lid of her trunk, then flung the strap of her gym bag over her shoulder. "Let me take these in, then I'll be ready to go."

"Come through the mudroom off the kitchen to the garage when you're ready," he instructed. "We'll be waiting for you."

Emma deposited her bags in Kayleigh's room, then wriggled her phone into the zippered armband before yanking it up to her bicep. Anxious to leave the confines of the house and their circular discussions behind, she hurried out to the garage. There, she found Kayleigh standing next to an expensive racing bike. It looked to be a slightly smaller version of her father's sleek ride. A more clunky-looking touring bike with wide tires stood on its kickstand nearby. Emma eyed the narrow saddles on the racing bikes and sent up a silent prayer of thanks when she compared them to the more substantial seat on the cruiser.

"Okay," she said as she stepped into the garage. "I call the bike with the complete seat."

Kayleigh expelled a mirthless laugh. "It's all yours." She swung one long leg over the crossbar of the racing bike and plunked a sleek black helmet on her head.

"The only spare helmet I had was Kayleigh's old one," Max explained, nodding to the sparkling pink hard-shell dangling from the cruiser's handlebars.

Determined to play it cool, Emma shrugged off his apology. "I like sparkles." Feigning a comfort level she didn't feel, she placed the helmet on her head and tightened the strap. "It's been a while since I've ridden a bike, so I'll probably be bringing up the rear, but don't worry—I'll have your six."

"Now, remember, the right hand brake is for the rear wheel. Try not to use the front brakes on any downhill inclines," Max instructed.

Emma huffed a laugh as she secured the strap under her chin. "I said it'd been a while, but I don't think I've forgotten the fundamentals. What's the old bit about things being like riding a bike?"

Max smiled and strapped his own helmet on, then nodded to his daughter. "Lead the way," he said with a wave. "We'll head down by the park then pick up dinner on our way back. Sound good?"

"Sounds fabulous," Kayleigh said with a hint of sass. "Try to keep up," she called over her shoulder, pushing off.

Max waited until Emma raised the kickstand and pushed off herself before mounting his bike. He caught up to her before she even found her balance. They rode side by side on the quiet residential street, Emma feeling self-conscious with every downward stroke of the pedal. "I didn't mean to be rude earlier." She darted a glance in his direction. "About why you came to Simon," she clarified.

"You weren't wrong," he replied, not the least bit winded.

Emma leaned into the handlebars and pushed harder as they started up an incline. "So how do you know Simon?"

"College. We were assigned to be roommates our freshman year in the dorms."

She glanced over at him. "Really?" she huffed, her breath coming out choppy. "Random assignment?"

"Yep."

She heard the *click-click-click* of his gears changing, but was too focused on making it to the top to look over at him.

"The guy I was supposed to room with took off to be a surfer in Costa Rica over the summer. I walked into my room and there sat this scrawny guy from a town I'd never heard of, already typing away at his computer. I remember his whole half of the room was already set up. Everything in place. The clothes in the closet, books stacked on the shelf, everything in its place," he said with a laugh.

"Sounds like Simon," she huffed.

"Let's say I wasn't surprised to see how clean his office at headquarters was."

Emma smiled at the dryness of his tone. "And you two have stayed friends all these years?"

"Yeah," Max said, sounding almost as surprised as she was by the notion. "He's a different kind of guy, but he's a good guy. He says what he means, and he means what he says. You don't meet a lot of people like him in life."

Emma forced a tremulous smile as she pushed to the top of the nearly nonexistent hill. "Oh. I'm pretty sure Simon was the prototype for a straight shooter." She treated herself to three deep breaths before she attempted to speak again. "In every way," she added. "Did you know he's an expert marksman?"

"No. But I can't say I'm surprised," Max said offhandedly. "Simon's the kind of guy who strives to be an expert in anything he finds interesting."

"True." Emma stopped pumping the pedals and allowed herself to coast as the momentum carried them downhill. "I swear I'm not this out of shape," she said with a rueful laugh. "I run." Then, remembering she hadn't run for the last few months, she heaved a sigh. "Or, I guess I should say I *was* a runner. I tore my Achilles tendon a few months ago, and I haven't been great about getting back on the streets."

"I understand. I wiped out on some loose gravel a couple years ago and messed my knee up pretty bad," he said gruffly. "I didn't really get back on the bike until about eight months ago."

Emma tipped up her chin, enjoying the feel of the warm spring air on her cheeks. "What got you over the hump?" she asked when the road flattened enough to require some effort on her part.

"Kayleigh." He tossed the answer off as if it should have been obvious to her. "She volunteered to help her friend Tia train for a triathlon. Of course, she needed a racing bike and the one I had was too tall…" He trailed off and she glanced over in time to catch his wry smile.

She laughed. "How horrified was she when you went out and bought a matched set?"

"I'd say about a seven out of ten."

Kayleigh, whom they'd caught up to on the incline, shook her head. "More like a nine, Daddy," she called out without looking over her shoulder.

Max laughed then stood up on his pedals and accelerated enough to catch up with his daughter with a few powerful pushes. "What did you say, slowpoke?"

Emma didn't have to see Kayleigh's face to know the girl responded with her usual eye roll. "I'm not racing you," she insisted, even as she leaned over her handlebars and started pedaling faster.

"You'd only lose," he taunted, then took off, his legs pumping like pistons.

The man clearly knew his child well, because Kayleigh took off after him with a shout of delighted frustration. Emma stuck to her original pace. She saw no sense in chasing after them. This wasn't a protective detail. At least, not in the sense where she was supposed to be anybody's bodyguard.

Happy to have a bit of time to herself, she leaned back, happy to enjoy a more leisurely ride to the park they'd agreed to use as their turnaround point. Her phone vibrated in her armband, but she didn't stop to check it. Whatever it was would have to wait another ten minutes.

By the time she cruised around a corner and spotted the park a few blocks away, her natural cop paranoia had crept back in enough to make her anxious to catch sight of the Hugheses again. She spotted the father and daughter stopped near the gates marking the entrance to the walking paths. They were talking to a tall, slender woman clad in skimpy running shorts and one of those tank tops with the crisscrossing straps.

Emma coasted up the curb, trying to decipher the messages telegraphed by the trio's body language.

The woman leaned forward as she spoke, her stance more insistent than aggressive. Max stood astride his bike, his face grave. He seemed to be pulling back, as if he wanted to put as much space as possible between himself and the woman. Kayleigh, bless her adolescent heart, didn't bother to mask her annoyance. Her cheeks were red. *Exertion or temper?* Emma wondered as she gently drew closer. The other woman's expression was taut as she said, "...from your account."

She squeezed the hand brake and the squeak of rubber on metal rims punctuated the threesome's tense conversation. A look of undisguised irritation flashed on the stranger's face when she realized Emma intended to stop beside them. Emma squinted in return, suddenly cursing her cavalier attitude toward missed messages on her phone. Was one of the team trying to alert her to an issue?

"Hey," she said, blandly returning the stranger's glare as she inserted herself into their conversation. "Sorry it took me so long."

"Emma, this is Amy Birch," Max said, gesturing to the spandex-clad woman. "She's a teacher at Kayleigh's school." He turned to the teacher and tipped his head to the side. "This is Emma Parker. She's—"

"My aunt," Kayleigh interjected, causing Max to jolt.

"Uh, um," he said weakly.

Emma blinked twice, but remained silent as she raised a hand to her forehead to wipe away both her perspiration and confusion.

"My mom's sister," Kayleigh explained, warming to her story. "She's staying with us for a bit."

"Oh, how, uh, nice," Amy Birch replied, glancing from the tall, willowy teen to Emma, her brow furrowed.

Irked by the other woman's natural skepticism, Emma

doubled down on the teen's tale. "Yep. Kay-kay's my girl," she said in an overly chipper tone. "She inherited the Hughes height, of course. The Parker genes were totally recessive," she said, waving a hand toward her shorter, sturdier legs.

"Ms. Birch teaches Information Technology," Kayleigh informed her. Before Emma could comment on the information, she plowed ahead. "Auntie Em here is a computer genius, too."

"Is she?" Amy Birch lifted a single skeptical eyebrow.

"Oh, no," Emma replied with a scoff. "Data analysis. Nothing exciting."

"So, uh, we should let you get back to your run. Good seeing you," Max interjected. He turned to look directly at Emma and she read a clear plea in the man's eyes. "If we're going to pick up dinner on the way home, we should get to it." He moved his bike back and gestured toward the running path as if inviting her to take the lead.

"Right." She flashed a polite smile as she mentally captured the dozens of questions zipping around in her head and stuffed them into a box to be trotted out later. "Nice to meet you."

Amy Birch pressed her tongue to the inside of her upper lip as if she was having trouble holding back questions of her own, but in the end opted to swallow them. She lifted a hand in a casual wave. "Yes, I should…" She darted one more glance at Max, then turned to his daughter. "Hope to see you back in school soon, Kayleigh."

"Thanks, Ms. Birch," Kayleigh called after her in a gratingly chipper tone, as the woman took off.

"What was that?" Emma asked, trying to figure out the undercurrent of the conversation she'd interrupted. "What was she saying?"

"Let's talk at home," Max said gruffly.

Unwilling to be put off so easily, Emma turned to Kayleigh. "What happened?"

The teenager lifted one shoulder then let it fall. "Nothing."

When both Emma and her father shot her exasperated stares, she huffed. "She said there'd been more posts. Accused Dad of not 'monitoring my online activities' closely enough," she said, fingers curling into air quotes and words dripping with disdain.

"Let's head home," Max said, his jaw hardening.

"I'm not going to hide for the rest of my life," Kayleigh said, her own face settling into the same hard lines as her father's. "I didn't start this drama."

"It's hardly been two days," Max reminded her. "And a girl who was once a good friend of yours tried to hurt herself over all this drama, so spare me your attitude, please." He pulled his phone from his pocket and tapped around on the screen.

"Did she say what the posts said?"

"I don't want to talk about it here," Max said through clenched teeth.

Emma glanced around at the park filled with after-work joggers, cyclists and children at play. "Fine. You order and I'll pick it up."

"I know Kay and I will be having the Paradise Bowl," he said, head down as he jabbed at the screen with a tad too much force. "Do you know what you'd like, or do you need a menu?" he asked without a glance in Emma's direction.

"What's in the Paradise Bowl?" she asked.

"Everything," Kayleigh answered, sliding into a sulk. "I'm going to head home," she said, then pushed off without waiting for a response.

Max looked up from the screen, but Emma stopped him from calling out to her with a hand on his forearm. "Let her get a head start. She needs a minute."

"I need a minute," he grumbled.

"Did she say what the messages said?" Emma asked in a low voice.

"More of the same. Picking on different kids," he answered without looking up from his phone. The device chimed, and he looked up. "There. I set it up under your name, but it's all paid for," he informed her as he settled his foot against a pedal.

"You don't have to—"

"It's done." The note of frustrated finality in his tone made her swallow the rest of her protest. "I need to at least keep her in sight," he said, preparing to push off.

Nodding her understanding, Emma leaned back, giving him plenty of room to push off. "Go. It'd be better if you don't have to see me walking this thing up the last big hill."

The corner of his mouth kicked up, but he didn't say anything else. She stood rooted to the spot, enjoying the view as he rocked the bike back and forth in an effort to gain momentum. The second he was out of sight, she unzipped her armband and pulled her phone free.

There were three message bubbles from Simon Taylor.

Dawson tells me U have a pin drop on the sender's location.

Will have to discuss next steps.

More messages on subject's alt PicturSpam account. Last post 30 mins ago. Confirm bogus. Assigning Ross to help with SM.

Emma grunted. He was assigning another agent to monitor social media? Did he think she couldn't handle this case?

She replied: Off site with H's atm, but 99% sure bogus. Will confirm on return.

Without waiting for a reply, she zipped the phone back into its pocket and turned her bike in the direction of the restaurant. When she arrived, she parked the cruiser near the entrance, feeling uneasy about her inability to secure it with a lock. The kid behind the to-go counter confirmed the order and told her it would be another few minutes. Settling into a corner of the waiting area, she alternated between watching the bike and the steady stream of athlesiure-clad diners lining up for a table.

When her phone buzzed, she jumped, then fumbled with the zipper again. She unlocked the device only to find another text from her boss.

Dawson confirmed messaged posted using browser, not mobile app. Talked to Blanton abt equip. Mainly tablets. Some tchrs have laps, but most use tabs. Abt a dzn towers in IT lab.

Emma blinked as the image of the woman she'd met in the park mere minutes before flashed into her mind. She'd been dressed for running but had not broken a sweat. And the way she looked at Max and Kayleigh Hughes niggled at her.

The tiny vestibule filled with hungry customers chatting about their days and grumbling about the wait. She closed her eyes, trying to capture the image of Amy Birch in her mind before moving back to logistics.

"Parker?" the young man who'd greeted her called above the din.

Emma jumped to her feet and threaded her way through the waiting diners to snag the brown paper to-go bag he extended in her direction. "Thanks," she called, then murmured, "Excuse me" over and over again as she beat a path to the door.

The relief she felt when she spotted the bike sitting right where she left it nearly made her laugh out loud. The last thing she wanted was pull up to the Hughes house in a rideshare. Max was trusting her with his daughter's future. It would be hard to maintain credibility if she lost his bicycle.

She threaded the handles of the bag through the handlebars then threw her leg over. Straddling the crossbar, she took a minute to reply.

I'll pick Kayleigh's brain about which teachers use laptops, lab setup for the IT department and student access outside of class time.

After slipping the phone back into its compartment, she yanked up the zipper. Eyeing the narrow sidewalk running along the busy through street, she weighed her options for her return to the Hughes home. The thoroughfare would be more direct and slightly less hilly, but they were in the thick of evening traffic and there was no bike lane available on this particular stretch. Resigned, she pointed the bike in the direction of the residential streets.

As she huffed her way up the final hill, she had bargained her way up to four days per week lifting weights in the gym at headquarters, in addition to her vow to get back into her running routine. She coasted up the gracefully curving drive breathless and beyond dewy, only to find Max leaning against the trunk of her car, his arms crossed over his chest.

"Did you think I took off with your dinner?" she asked, brakes squeaking as she drew to a halt beside him.

"Nah. I'd hope if you were going to indulge in food theft it would be something more exciting than salad."

"You know it," she said, lifting the bag off her bike and handing it over to him.

He smiled as he took it from her. She dismounted and without another glance over her shoulder, she pushed the bike toward the garage. "I want it noted for the record I pushed through every one of those hills."

"So noted."

He followed her into the three-car garage. Once again, she marveled at the pristine polished concrete floor and perfectly organized storage containers of holiday decorations lining the back wall, wondering how people managed to keep their spaces so clean. She was lucky she had a basket of clean laundry handy when she swung by her apartment.

"Here," he said, extending the to-go bag. "Trade me."

She was all too happy to exchange the bike for the bag. "How do you do this?" she asked, unable to hold back her curiosity.

"Do what?" His biceps flexed and she tried her best not to stare as he gripped the bike by the bars and seat, then swung it easily up over his head. She gaped as he lifted it onto a couple of heavy duty hooks drilled into the garage ceiling. Only then did she notice the racing bikes hanging suspended above a white Jeep with a removable soft top.

"Your house is so clean."

He dusted his hands off on his shorts. "I have cleaners come every two weeks to do the big stuff, but it's only me and Kay, so it's not hard to keep up with stuff from one day to another."

Emma was grateful this man who made everything he did look so easy would never have cause to see her mess of a one-bedroom apartment. She rustled the bag. "Come on, I have some questions."

"Of course you do." He rolled his eyes, and father and daughter had never looked more alike.

"I'm a cop. Asking questions is what I do," she answered, happy to fall back into the comfortable pattern of police work. He gestured for her to precede him into the house and a flash of subconscious insight she'd been trying to unearth popped fully into focus.

She halted on the step leading into the mudroom and turned back to look him straight in the eyes. "You know, I couldn't help picking up on something more than a parent-teacher vibe going on back there."

"What? Back where?" he asked, brow puckering.

"In the park," she clarified, undeterred by his obfuscation. "But Kayleigh didn't seem to get it, so before we go in there, I think you'd better tell me how you know Amy Birch."

# *Chapter Eight*

Max knew the question was coming, but her matter-of-fact approach still startled him. He was accustomed to the thrust and parry of so-called polite conversation. He should have expected it. Anyone who worked for Simon would have to be as blunt as he was.

"After dinner," he said in a near whisper.

Her eyes widened, but she walked past him into the house without pushing the point any further. For some reason her reticence made him even more nervous.

In the kitchen he busied himself with unpacking the to-go containers while Emma and Kayleigh bonded by complaining about the bike ride. He kept his back to them, pushing the packs of plastic utensils aside in favor of using the real deal, and fished the packets of dressing from the depths of the bag.

"Kay, will you get drinks, please?" he asked as he deposited a bowl in front of each of them.

"I'm having water," she announced as she slid off her stool. "Emma? Water? Milk? A Coke?"

"Water's fine," Emma replied, her gaze following him as he arranged napkins and forks.

"Me, too, please," Max said, placing his own bowl in front of the stool on the other side of Kayleigh. He wanted to maintain a buffer between him and this uncomfortable conversation as long as possible. But any thoughts he may have had about a relaxing meal evaporated as soon as his daughter started in on her meal prep.

"So have you looked?" she asked Emma as she squeezed the contents of an entire dressing packet over her bowl.

"At the new posts? Not yet, but Wyatt said he was sending over metadata on them. I'll study it after we eat."

Kayleigh gave her salad a stir with her fork, then set aside the utensil. She snapped the plastic lid back onto the bowl, flipped it over and shook it over her head, turning the artfully arranged contents into a jumble. "What will the metadata tell you?" she asked as she pried off the lid again.

"Like any data set, metadata contains all sorts of information. We'll start with the most basic stuff. Where, when and how it was posted—"

"I think you're forgetting who," Max grumbled. The easy rapport Kayleigh and Emma had developed in one day irked him. He couldn't remember the last time his daughter was this curious about anything he did, and it made him feel peevish. Petulant.

"I never forget the who," Emma answered evenly, jolting him out of his sulk. "But if I go off the data visible to the untrained eye, the 'who' is sitting right next to me," she said, pointing the tines of her fork at Kayleigh. She leaned forward to cock a victorious eyebrow at him, then sat back before continuing. "That's why we can't take data at face value. It's easily manipulated."

"Then why is gathering more of it so important?" Kayleigh persisted.

"Because gathering a whole bunch of clues is better than picking one up and running with it," Emma replied easily. "There's bound to be some garbage in the pile, fake accounts, IP masking and the like, but it's possible to build a solid foundation with even the shakiest material. Like how if you use sand and pebbles to fill in the gaps, you can build a wall out of round rocks," she said, gesturing with her fork as she spoke. "More information can make a case stronger."

The three of them lapsed into silence. Kayleigh shoveled in the food as if she was in a contest, but Max noticed Emma seemed to like to ponder as she ate. A few minutes passed before Kayleigh spoke up.

"Will you show them to me?"

The vulnerability the question exposed made him want to say "No, absolutely not," but before he could figure out a more palatable way to lay down the law with his stubborn almost-grown child, Emma Parker pulled her phone from the neoprene sleeve strapped to her arm.

"Sure. Let's look at them together." She made the suggestion with a gentleness Max knew would undercut any edict he might issue.

Peeved, he fell back to his last line of defense: house rules.

"No devices during dinner," he blurted.

Both women turned to look at him, incredulous. "Dad—" Kayleigh began, but he shook his head hard.

"I'm serious. I'd like to eat my stupid, overpriced spinach salad in peace, if you don't mind."

Emma placed her phone face down on the island, and the three of them went back to eating in silence. Kayleigh stabbed a plump olive glistening with dressing and held it up as if it was proof he was losing his mind. "There's more than spinach in here. Such drama."

"He's right. We'll look at them later. I'll show you both what we're looking at and how we dissect it all." He watched as Emma used her fork to move some of the diced tomato away from the carefully arranged line of cubed chicken before she plowed her way through the protein section of her dinner.

"It's better if you mix it all up," Kayleigh suggested helpfully.

"Not everyone shares your appreciation for food chaos,

Kay," Max said as he watched his daughter decimate her dinner in record time.

"Fine," she said as she scraped together one last forkful. "You guys poke around and have your 'peaceful dinner,'" she said, using finger quotes. "I'm going to go shower," she announced, pushing her chair back without waiting for any reply.

She rinsed the plastic bowl and lid before placing them in the recycling, then dropped her fork into the dishwasher. Leaning onto the island opposite Emma, Kayleigh waited impatiently until the government agent looked up from her careful picking.

"You will show me, won't you?"

She fixed Emma with a stubborn glare so similar to his late wife's that it made his breath tangle in his chest.

Emma nodded solemnly. "I will because I think you have a right to know what's out there, but I want you to think long and hard about whether you want to see the actual posts while you shower. I'll tell you what you allegedly posted, but I don't think it would be good for you to read any of the comments," she said bluntly. "You know how bad it can be."

Kayleigh straightened and drummed the pads of her fingers lightly on the edge of the island. "Okay. I'll think about it."

The minute she left the room, Emma pushed away her bowl and swung her legs in his direction. "Okay. Give me the story."

He tried to buy some time by peering into her bowl. "Not a fan of tomatoes?"

"Not one bit."

"Aren't you going to eat your olives?"

"Not if you paid me." She pushed the bowl across the marble surface. "Take what you want."

Max reached for the remains of her salad, happy for the distraction. He scraped the tomatoes, cucumbers and olives into his own bowl, then set hers aside with a sigh. "Last summer I tried to use one of those, uh, dating apps."

"A dating app," she repeated, leveling him with a steady gaze.

Unable to meet her eyes, he focused on picking his favorite bits out of the bowl. "We matched and met up for coffee. She said she was a teacher, but we hadn't met before, so I didn't think much about it." He sighed and popped a hummus-dipped olive into his mouth, buying time as he chewed.

"You didn't know she was a teacher at Capitol Academy?" she persisted, piecing together the bits he wasn't saying while he stalled.

"She wasn't yet. We were on our second coffee, uh, date when she mentioned starting at a private school in the fall. When I found out she was going to be at CA, I ended the date."

She eyed him curiously. "Ended it how?"

"What do you mean *how*?" he asked, uncomfortable with this line of questioning.

"You know, did you get up and storm out, leaving her with the check and your half-eaten biscotti?" She held up a hand. "No, wait. You said you'd call, but then ghosted her."

He reared back, startled by the scenarios she'd cooked up and what each one seemed to say about him. "I told her my daughter was a student at Capitol Academy, and that I was heavily involved with the school. I didn't think the two of us continuing to see one another was wise. She agreed."

Emma exhaled her disappointment, then shrugged. "Boring but effective," she assessed. "Did you sense any ill will on her part? Did she try to talk you around? Try to keep the relationship going?"

"What?" He shook his head. "No. It wasn't a relationship, it was two coffee dates. One and a half, really. And she didn't want the complication any more than I did," he insisted, pointing at her with his fork before dropping it into his bowl.

"Hey, I'm only trying to look at this from every angle," she said, raising her hands in defense.

"I understand, but there's nothing more to read into it. I

spent a couple hours chatting with the woman in a public place almost eight months ago."

"Gotcha." She pushed back from the counter and began gathering her things. But she wasn't done with him. Not by a long shot. "I'm only asking if there's any way she could have a different perspective on things. I mean, you're a, uh, nice-looking guy," she said as she ran water in the sink. "Nice house. Nice clothes. Nice car…"

Max blinked, taken aback by both the implication he was a catch and her repeated use of the word *nice*. Why did it sound like a condemnation when used more than twice in a sentence and never once applied to any aspect of his personality?

"You think she's been silently harboring some kind of crush on me?"

"Is it such a wild assumption?"

"It is a bit out there. You think she's trying to get my attention by ruining my daughter's prospects?" He shook his head, unable to entertain the notion. "What was posted today?"

"I haven't looked yet, but they posted after school hours from somewhere on the school property."

"Can you pull up the accounts here?" he asked, nodding to her phone.

Emma nodded and picked up her phone. With practiced ease, she swiped and tapped until she was in one of the PicturSpam accounts with his daughter's user photo. There were hundreds of comments under the photo his daughter had posted days before. Emma opened the thread and jumped expertly to the latest comments.

@MiklMomo2029: I hear @kayleighhughes08's daddy chked her into rehab.

@LindC: You mean Zaddy Hugebucks is home alone? Hold my macchiato.

@ITgrrl7789: Rehab 4 wut? Personality transplant?

@LindC: They still live up on the hill, rite?

@MiklMomo2029: Ha! U heading over @LindC? You'll have to beat up all the PTA moms to get near him. Incl urs.

@LindC: Tell UR daddy I sed hi, @MiklMomo2029.

@ITgrrl7789: Like @kayleighhughes08's hot dad will look twice at a girl his kid's age. Guy's got ETHICS.

@LindC: *gasp* @ITgrrl7789 Noooooo! Is there a shot for that?

@ITgrrl7789: Sadly no cure

He frowned, perplexed by the commentary. "Are they talking about me?"

"Yep. You're the zaddy," she said, swiping out of the app. "These are the nicer ones. PicturSpam has pretty strict user guidelines. People are freer on sites like ChitChat, where they think their posts are protected."

"Protected from whom?"

"They have restricted audiences. The user can choose who sees their commentary in their feeds," she explained.

"How'd you get in?" He turned his curious gaze on her as she scrolled. Emma looked up, her eyes sparkling with amusement.

"I'm magic."

"You're a hacker," he countered.

"Of a sort," she admitted. "But I work for the good guys." She turned her attention back to her screen and jabbed at it a few times. "Well, would you look at…"

"What?"

She turned the phone toward him. "Our friend at-ITgrrl-seven-seven-eight-nine is on Chit, too. I need to let Wyatt know. We're cross-referencing the handles used on various platforms. Doesn't mean anything definitive. People can use different profile names and have multiple accounts, but it's worth a try. Most people are pretty lazy when it comes to usernames and passwords."

She switched to her messaging app and typed out a message with her thumbs. When she was done, she huffed a strand of hair away from her forehead and toggled back to the ChitChat screen. "Let's see what she has to say."

He peered over her shoulder as she scrolled through post after post complaining about Kayleigh, ugly things his daughter allegedly said or did to "friends" or "someone I know," and a passel of speculation about Kayleigh's car, wardrobe, spending. His cheeks flamed as he realized a number of comments referred to him bankrolling Kayleigh's lavish lifestyle and referring to him with various money-related nicknames.

"I think this user is obsessed with you," Emma murmured as she continued to read. "Do you think her handle is 'it' girl, or 'IT' girl," she asked, turning wide, questioning eyes on him. "Maybe an IT teacher?"

"You think this is…?" He let the question trail away. "No." He stepped back, needing to put some space between himself and the notion of Amy Birch participating in—or perpetrating—this assault on Kayleigh's reputation.

"Not possible?" she challenged.

"It wasn't anything more than coffee," he insisted.

"For you." She closed out of the app. "I'm floating a theory."

"It's pretty out there."

"But worth pursuing, in my opinion. I think I'll set up a coffee date with Ms. Birch."

"I think you'd better clear it with Kayleigh first," he said, crossing his arms over his chest.

"Why?"

"Because, for some mysterious reason she decided to promote you to Aunt Emma, remember?"

She blinked twice and her forehead puckered. "Oh, yeah. Why did she?"

He shrugged. "No clue, but she must have had some reason. You'll need to talk to her."

"I will." She gave a decisive nod as she peeled the empty phone sleeve from her arm. "But even if she doesn't want me to blow her cover story for me, I can still reach out. You know, as a concerned aunt. One IT professional to another," she added with a small smirk.

EMMA SPENT THE evening holed up in Kayleigh's room. When not on the phone with other members of the Cyber Crime Division, she was quizzing his daughter about social-media handles and the intricate and interwoven connections between the teenagers mentioned in various posts. He'd lingered outside Kayleigh's door a couple times, listening to them talk. The two of them had slipped into the sort of easy back-and-forth he hadn't enjoyed with his daughter in years.

Feeling out of sorts and generally left out, he retreated to his home office and placed a call to Emma Parker's boss.

Simon answered on the first ring. "Taylor here."

"Hughes," Max countered.

"How's it going?" his old friend asked absently.

"You tell me."

"Good," Simon answered without hesitation. "Things are good."

"Really?" Max gave an incredulous snort. "Have you seen some of these posts?"

"I've seen the ones the team has flagged," Simon replied.

"How many total?"

"Uh, hang on." There was a rustling followed by the sound of keystrokes. "I think I've made it through about two hundred and sixty-seven."

Max sat up in his chair. "What?"

"Two hundred and sixty-seven," Simon repeated.

"Posts from Kayleigh's accounts?" he asked, stunned.

"From the accounts we've flagged as using her likeness or referencing her username."

Max scrubbed a hand over his eyes. He had no idea the situation had grown so out of hand. "So many?"

Simon grunted. "There are a lot more. These are the ones my team has flagged as being of particular interest."

"By what criteria?"

"We always tag any communications containing threatening, defamatory or accusatory language. Then we start looking for patterns—mentions, users, linguistic ticks."

"Linguistic ticks?" Max repeated with a scoff.

"You'd be surprised how much we can figure out by analyzing patterns of speech, colloquialisms, online shorthand. All forms of communication contain a signature, even if they don't attach a name."

"You have never sounded nerdier," Max muttered, using his thumb and forefinger to massage the bridge of his nose.

"In this case, my nerdiness is exactly what you need."

Max smiled tiredly. Simon was right. His old friend's dispassionate analysis was exactly what he needed at the moment. "So this is progress?"

"This is leaps and bounds," Simon assured him. "Trust me."

"I do."

"Emma's doing okay with Kayleigh?"

Max slumped in his seat again, thinking about the snarky cackles of laughter he'd heard drifting into the hall. "They're getting along great."

There was a momentary pause. "Jealous?"

Max pursed his lips. The accuracy of Simon's question landed like a punch to the gut. For a man with few social skills, his old friend had a knack for cutting straight through to a person's emotional core. But Simon wasn't any good with anything that oozed out of those soft, sticky centers.

"A little," he said, knowing Simon would see through any attempt to deflect.

"You know she'll always need you," his friend said in his usual matter-of-fact tone.

"Maybe I want to be wanted, not needed."

The words escaped him before he could think them through. But Simon never judged when someone expressed their feelings. Max had long suspected it was because his friend seemed to be truly baffled by emotion.

When the silence stretched too long, Max heaved a sigh of defeat. "Are the posts bad?"

"Compared to some of the stuff we see? Nothing shocking."

Max bristled at his friend's lack of empathy. "Well, we're not all animatronic cops. Would a human being find them shocking?"

As ever, Simon remained unperturbed by the sarcasm. "Emma thinks it may be an adult. Kids don't usually acknowledge the existence of parents, much less comment on them," he said. "She tells me you dated the Information Technology teacher last year."

"I didn't date her, I went on a date with her," he clarified. "Coffee."

"Emma said you met her twice."

"Don't you two have anything germane to the case to discuss?"

"You dated and rejected someone with what I assume would be a fairly substantial tech background to be teaching at a school like CA. I'd say it's relevant to an investigation into the pervasive hacking and spoofing of your daughter's electronics."

"I can't believe an adult would purposefully taunt teenagers into self-harm," Max insisted.

"Another reason why you're not a cop. You aren't suspicious enough," Simon concluded. "Emma's going to set up a meeting with the teacher."

"Fine." Max leaned forward in his chair, prepared to abandon it and this conversation. "I'll let you get back to your sleuthing."

"She knows what she's doing," Simon said. "Trust her. If there's anyone who can connect with Kayleigh, it's Emma."

"I know. I'll talk to you later."

"Later," Simon replied distractedly.

Muted beeps signaled the end of the conversation. Max stared at the home screen on his phone, trying to swallow the cold lump of fear lodged in his throat. What if he was the reason this was happening? He thought back to the time he and Amy Birch met for coffee, trying to recall if there'd been any red flags.

She'd seemed perfectly nice. Normal. A woman who'd burned out on the corporate rat race and opted to use her skills to help others. They'd exchanged polite greetings at the school open house. She hadn't even requested a parent-teacher conference when Kayleigh had taken her class in the fall. When they discovered she'd be a teacher at Capitol, they'd mutually agreed it was better not to continue getting together. Had he totally misread her? Was it possible she'd been plotting and planning her revenge this whole time?

No.

He shook his head as he planted a hand on his desk and rose from his chair. He was willing to entertain the possibility of an adult causing all this harm and chaos, but he refused to believe Amy Birch was the one. He might not be a cop, but he knew how to read people. His job depended on him having a finely attuned sense of when someone was on the up-and-up.

As a venture capitalist, he was approached by entrepreneurs on a daily basis. Nearly every one of them would be willing to sell their grandmother for seed money. Most were wholeheartedly convinced their business was on the brink of breaking through. Few of them actually were, and even fewer actually survived beyond the brink.

He stalked in the direction of Kayleigh's bedroom. If the investigation was going to involve him, he'd be a part of the conversation whether or not he was welcome in the girls' club they'd formed.

But when he peered in through the open door, he saw only Emma seated on the bed, her computer on her lap, a tablet on the bedspread near her hip, a phone in her hand and another plugged into one of the laptop's ports. She had on earbuds and was drumming her forefinger on the wrist rest of the computer.

He cleared his throat, but it wasn't enough. She was reading a rapidly moving feed on the phone she held, her eyes darting back and forth at a feverish pace. He was about to step into the room when she frowned, captured whatever she'd seen on the phone's screen, then started typing into the computer, her fingers hitting the keys with thumping urgency.

"What is it?" he asked, but she remained oblivious, her frown deepening. "Emma?" He stepped into the room, but she kept typing, her gaze darting to the phone she'd dropped into her lap. He hesitated for a moment, then, when her typing slowed, he dropped heavily onto the side of the bed.

Her head popped up on a gasp. She blinked twice, then yanked the cord, pulling the buds from her ears. "You scared me."

"Sorry, I tried to get your attention," he said, gesturing vaguely toward the now empty doorway. Her hand settled on her throat and he saw the pulse beneath her jaw flutter beneath fair skin. "I'm sorry," he repeated.

"'S'okay," she said, sounding breathless. "I was… I was in deep, I guess." She picked up the phone and pressed the button to lock the screen.

"What happened?" he asked, nodding to the phone to let her know he'd witnessed whatever had upset her.

"Oh, I, uh," she stammered, glancing at her laptop screen, then back up again. "I'm following some of the chatter."

"You saw something. It upset you." He pinned her with a direct stare. "Was it about Kayleigh?"

She shook her head quickly enough to convince him. "Oh, no. Not Kayleigh."

He exhaled his relief, but Emma remained stiff, her brow pleated so tightly he reached up to smooth it.

They both jumped when his thumb made contact, and Max sprang from the bed. "Sorry," he blurted, his ears flaming. "I didn't mean—" He grimaced. "Force of habit. When Kayleigh gets upset, she gets the…" He trailed off, rubbing the spot between his own eyebrows.

She offered him a half-hearted smile. "Oh. No. No problem. I understand."

He shoved his hands deep into the pockets of his shorts, backed up another step and nearly toppled over the oversize faux-fur blob Kayleigh insisted on using in place of a real chair. "Jeez," he grumbled. "This place is like an obstacle course."

Emma chuckled and pushed herself up against the headboard. "Girls like their stuff." She gestured to the fluffy footstool. "I'm thinking of getting one for my place."

He lifted an eyebrow, impressed by her ability to pivot and deflect. "Uh-huh." He crossed his arms over his chest and tucked his chin. He liked to think of it as his I-mean-business stance, but was fairly sure it would have no more effect on

Emma than it did on Kayleigh. Still, he gave it a shot. "What upset you?"

"Some kids talking about another kid." She shrugged and made an attempt to wipe the worry from her face, but he held her gaze, not letting her off the hook. "Soon, I'll have an on-going correspondence with Dr. Blanton and Ms. Guthrie, the school counselor," she said, as if she'd explained everything with a single sentence.

"An ongoing correspondence about…?" he asked, raising a querying eyebrow.

"I screenshot posts I think may contain cause for concern," she informed him, an edge of defensiveness creeping into her voice.

"What kind of cause for concern?"

"Anything we think indicates a student may be a threat."

"To others or themselves?"

"Both."

"And what happens after you flag it?" he persisted.

"Dr. Blanton and Ms. Guthrie take it from there. I want to nip it in the bud before they do something to require police involvement." She gave him a sad smile. "In other words, I'm hoping I never meet any of these kids."

"Simon says you guys are thinking an adult is behind some of this."

Her smile twisted into a smirk. "Simon says."

Max chuckled. He couldn't count the number of times he and his friends had used the prompt from the old game to taunt the man himself. "You want to meet with Amy Birch," he said, pushing the point.

"I am meeting her. We're having coffee tomorrow morning," she informed him, tipping up her chin as if expecting him to retaliate. "Apparently, she has first period free."

But Max only nodded his approval. "Good. I'll come along."

She spluttered a laugh. "No."

"Yes," he countered.

"This is a police investigation," she reminded him.

"One started at my behest," he replied. "Don't make me go camp out in your back seat. I have a vested interest, and if your theories about her supposed interest in me hold any water, she'll be more helpful with me along."

Emma eyed him warily, gnawing the inside of her cheek as she weighed his argument. After a protracted minute, she gave in with a graceless shrug. "Suit yourself. We ride at oh-seven-thirty," she said, pointedly returning her attention to her screen.

"I'll be saddled up and ready to go." He tapped twice on the doorframe as he backed out of the room. "Do you want the door closed?" he asked.

"Please." Without another glance in his direction, she picked up the phone, scowled fiercely at the screen, then fired off another missive.

He closed the door behind him, wondering which of the dozens of children he'd watch grow up alongside his daughter would be the next target.

## Chapter Nine

Emma was up and ready to go early the next morning. She dressed in her usual work clothes—dark pants, a clean white shirt and her trusty loafers—and went into the attached bath to brush her hair.

Kayleigh appeared in the doorway as she was dusting her nose with powder foundation and asked, in the startling direct but genuinely curious way of teenagers, if she was trying *not* to look pretty. "I mean, you know, downplaying your best features because you work in a male-dominated field," she suggested as she propped a hip on the edge of the bathroom counter.

"Uh, no."

"Because you can help yourself to whatever," Kayleigh said, gesturing to the bounty of her cosmetics collection as if the two of them were girlfriends.

Frowning as she leaned closer to the mirror to apply a swipe of mascara, Emma shook her head. "I don't see the point of fussing with fifteen layers of stuff," Emma said with a shrug. "I'm not trying to impress anyone." She paused as she stepped back, biting her bottom lip as she inspected her reflection. "Why? You think I look bad?"

"I'm not saying you look bad," Kayleigh said in a rush. "I'm only asking because, I don't know... Maybe some lip gloss?"

She pulled a tube of berry-colored lip stain from a partitioned organizer and thrust it at Emma. "A touch of color."

Emma squeezed a bit onto her finger, then slicked it onto her lips. "There. Satisfied?" She stalked out of the en suite and grabbed her computer bag.

Kayleigh grinned so wide a dimple flashed in her cheek. "A thousand percent. Do you want to borrow a purse?" She gestured to the walk-in closet like a game-show hostess. "Perhaps something in a nice, boring black?"

Emma rolled her eyes as she draped the strap of the messenger bag across her body. A quick peek confirmed she had both her laptop and the small leather case containing her credentials. She dropped Kayleigh's tablet and cell into the bag before shoving her own into the outside pocket.

"Thanks, but I'm good as I am."

"Suit yourself." Kayleigh leaned against the doorjamb, her arms wrapped tight around her torso. "You don't trust me enough to leave my phone?"

Emma flashed her a sympathetic smile. "I do trust you, but I also have read about every study known to man about the dopamine hit people get when they check their socials, and I know how hard it is to resist temptation." She pointed to the laptop closed on the desk. "Do not log on."

Kayleigh shuddered, eyeballing the computer with a sneer. "As if I'm letting that creeper peek at me."

"Hang tight." She turned to leave the room. "We won't be gone long."

"You kids have fun now," Kayleigh called after her. "Say hi to Ms. Birch, Auntie Emma."

Grimacing at the reminder of Emma's deception the day before, she clamped her lips together to keep from rising to the bait. She was pleased to find Max waiting in the kitchen, one of those pristine white coffee mugs in his hand.

"Pregame?" he asked, lifting the cup.

She shook her head. "No, I'll wait. Thanks," she added. "We're having coffee shop coffee, so I'll hold out for three pumps of caramel and extra whip."

He inclined his head. "Understood."

"Are you sure you want to do this?"

He took a sip of his coffee, unperturbed. "Why wouldn't I?"

"It could be awkward," she pointed out.

"Don't see why it should be. What do I have to say to convince you there was truly nothing between me and Amy Birch?"

"I'm not sure it matters if there was anything or not," she said, choosing her words carefully. "This could be one of those situations where reality and wishful thinking collide."

"I assure you it is not." He gave her a lopsided smile. "But I'm taking the fact you refuse to believe it as a compliment."

Tired of the byplay and ready to get to her interview, she pointed to his mug. "Take it however you like, as long as you take it to go." She hooked the thumb over her shoulder. "Do you want me to drive or are you one of those guys who feel threatened when a woman is behind the wheel."

"I don't appreciate you trying to shame me with patriarchy first thing in the morning," he returned good-naturedly. "I'll have you know I'm used to riding shotgun. Kayleigh drives nearly everywhere we go together."

"Does she think your eyesight is failing?"

"She says my reaction times are not what they ought to be," he said gravely. "I find hers to be overdeveloped, but I prefer when she errs on the side of caution." He took a deep drink of his coffee, then turned and placed the mug in the sink. "Should hold me until we can get to the main event."

"And people say cops are caffeine junkies," she scoffed.

"When you've been a single parent as long as I have, you don't have much time for vices. I have exactly one, and you're not taking it away from me."

Emma held up both hands in surrender. "I wouldn't dream of it."

He followed her out to the driveway and made his way to the passenger side of her car without any further comment. Emma unlocked the doors with the remote, half waiting for him to come up with some excuse to drive himself, if not the both of them, the six blocks to the coffee shop where they'd be meeting Amy Birch.

Again, Max surprised her. He dropped into the passenger seat and reached for the seat belt before she deposited her messenger bag on the back floorboard.

He moved the seat back to accommodate his long legs, but made no attempt at precoffee small talk, nor did he try to adjust her radio settings. She slid him a sidelong glance.

"What's the game plan here?" he asked.

"What do you mean 'game plan'?" She glanced over at him and found him sitting upright, drumming his fingers on his knee as she navigated the twisting neighborhood streets.

"Do we do this like a good-cop, bad-cop thing?" he asked.

She snorted a laugh. "I don't see how we could, since only one of us is a cop," she replied dryly.

"You know what I mean. Am I Mr. Nice Guy and you're the tough Special Agent coming in to interrogate the suspect?"

"I'm not sure people would classify you as Mr. Nice Guy, but if you see yourself as one, who am I to debase you of the notion?"

"Ha," he said sarcastically. "I know at least three people who think I'm a nice guy. But seriously, how am I supposed to play this?"

"How about you play the concerned father, and I'll be the cop asking questions of a person of interest in an investigation," she said as she slowed to a stop at the bottom of the hill.

Turning to look at him, she gentled her tone. "This isn't a TV show, Max. My job is nothing like the way Hollywood shows it. There will be no exciting car chases or dramatic confrontations with criminal masterminds. This is real life, and in real life most investigations are boring. They involve hours of analyzing data and looking for correlations."

"We're going to interrogate a suspect," he countered.

She snorted. "I don't interrogate people, I interview them. Sometimes a subject may have something interesting to offer. A case can turn on nothing more than a slip of the tongue. Some tidbit that makes us think 'Hey, maybe I should look at this,' or 'Maybe we should revisit so-and-so as a suspect,' but nine times out of ten, it comes down to data and evidence."

"You're making me wonder why I got out of bed early," he said sardonically.

She checked the intersection then hooked her right turn, accelerating slowly. "I wish I could tell you it would be more exciting, but frankly, for my own sake, I'm happy with the way it is." Offering a wan smile, she admitted, "I like the boring cases. Surprises usually mean an investigation has gone sideways, and I don't care much for variables I can't control. My job may be dull, but it still has the potential to be dangerous."

They rode in silence for a moment, then, when she put her blinker on to signal the turn into the coffee shop's parking lot, he glanced over at her with a grin. "So you're saying I should play the good cop, right?"

She chuckled and aimed for one of the few empty spaces in the tiny lot. "Absolutely."

Capitol Café was packed. She scanned the room as they entered but failed to spot Amy Birch.

From his greater vantage point, Max spotted a table in the far corner of the room. He leaned down to speak directly into her ear. "Back corner. We may have to snag a chair from another table, though," he said, indicating the small round table nestled against the wall.

"You go grab it, I'll get our coffees," she said, standing on her toes in an effort to reach his ear.

Max shook his head. "No, I'm the one crashing this party. I promised you a triple shot of caramel and croissants," he reminded her. "I'll keep an eye out for Amy and get her order before I send her back to you."

Biting her lower lip, Emma surveyed the crowded room, then nodded her acquiescence. Gesturing for him to lean down again, she stretched to shout over the din. "Three shots of caramel and extra whip," she reminded him.

"Yes, ma'am," he answered with a cheeky salute.

Holding her bag close to her body, she wove her way through the chattering morning crowd. She had no idea there were so many perky people in this town. Most mornings, it was all Emma could do to roll out of bed in time to splurge on fast-food coffee rather than drinking the sludge at headquarters.

A couple at a nearby table relinquished their spare chair in a flurry of smiles and waves. Uncaffeinated as she was, Emma did her best to plaster a cordial expression on her face as she laid claim to the table no one wanted.

The second she sat down, she understood why. Whoever opted for the corner seat would be hemmed in. Shifting to the chair on the opposite side of the table, she made a mental note to tell Max to leave the corner seat for Amy Birch. She might not be an expert in interrogation, but even Emma understood the advantage of putting a suspect's back to the wall.

Emma groped in the pocket of her bag for a pen. The place was too noisy to get a decent recording of their conversation, and she didn't want to spend the whole time typing notes into her laptop. She needed to get a good read on this woman, and she couldn't do so if she wasn't able to watch her as they spoke. Her fingers closed around a pen, and she sighed with relief. She placed her small notebook on the sticky tabletop, then twisted in her seat to check the line at the front.

Max was still three customers from the front of the line when Amy Birch breezed through the door. Emma watched as she drew up short and scanned the packed room. Confused recognition flashed across the other woman's face as their gazes met, but then Max must have called her name, because the other woman tore her gaze away.

Emma took the opportunity to observe the two of them together. Though Max leaned in close, like he had with her, she could tell it was merely to compensate for the noise in the room rather than any desire for intimacy. For her part, Amy Birch held her ground. She neither moved in closer nor backed away. The expression on her face and the confused glances she kept sending Emma's way told her the other woman felt she had been duped in some way. And in a way, she had.

When Emma had asked Kayleigh why she had introduced her as Aunt Emma, Kayleigh stuck with the story about explaining why Emma was staying in their house. But after today, it wouldn't be necessary. There was no reason for her to stay with the Hugheses any longer.

Besides, the whole aunt thing wouldn't hold water now. She wondered if the teacher was putting the pieces together. Emma watched as the other woman wove her way through the tables. She was pretty with her caramel-highlighted light brown hair and tortoiseshell glasses. Emma could see why any man would swipe right for a chance to meet Amy Birch.

"Special Agent Parker?" She injected each word with a healthy dose of skepticism.

Emma rose from her seat and extended her hand. As they shook, she flashed the teacher a rueful smile. "Yes. I'm Emma Parker." She pointed to the chair in the corner. "Have a seat. Is Max getting your drink order?"

Amy settled her handbag into her lap and nodded. "Yes,

thank you. I don't have much time before I have to be on campus."

Emma nodded. "Understood."

"Kayleigh said you worked in data analysis," she said, a puzzled frown rippling her brow.

Emma busied herself with her notepad and pen. She'd been the one to put a truthful spin on Kayleigh's fabrication about their relationship to one another, but Emma didn't see the point in correcting the record at this point. "Yes, I'm a data analyst for the Arkansas State Police."

"Would you mind if I asked to see some ID?" the other woman asked, clearly miffed at being misled.

"Not at all." She fished her credentials from her bag, opened the leather wallet and slid her badge and identification card across the sticky table.

She sat back, giving the other woman as much time as she needed to feel satisfied. At last, Amy spoke without looking up. "I assume you've been looking into some of these social-media posts Kayleigh's been making."

"Kayleigh isn't making those posts."

The statement came from above them as both women looked to find Max towering over the table, three cardboard-sleeved cups caught between his fingers. He bent to place them on the table. He slid a cup in front of Emma. "We have reason to believe someone has cloned Kayleigh's accounts."

Emma ducked her head to hide the smile tugging at the corner of her mouth. How easily he'd picked up on the terminology. She marveled at his ability to adapt. Was it something he picked up being a single parent for so long?

"Cloned?" Amy echoed as she accepted her drink. Clutching her cup, she fell back against the wooden slats of the chair. "I can't believe I didn't think about someone hacking her accounts," she said almost to herself.

"You didn't?" Emma asked.

The other woman's eyes snapped to hers. "Of course not. I mean, I had no reason to believe they weren't legitimate."

Emma could feel Max bristle even as he settled into the chair between them, but thankfully he said nothing.

Emma picked up her pen and pretended to jot a note on her pad. "You think Kayleigh is the type to post hateful things about other students? Have you witnessed a tendency to bully others in your interactions with her?"

Amy blinked, clearly caught out by the question. "Well, no. Nothing in particular," she conceded. "I guess I meant she's one of the more popular students. You know the kind of power popular kids have. The other girls look up to her. Want to dress like her, drive a car like hers and all those things. Sometimes being the one people envy and emulate doesn't bring out the best in a person's personality." She cast an apologetic glance in Max's direction. "Kayleigh seemed to have it all. Brains, beauty, money…" She shrugged as she trailed off.

"But you haven't witnessed any behavior you would consider aggressive or derogatory on Kayleigh's part?"

The other woman shook her head. "No."

"But you had no problem believing she would bully another student," Emma said flatly.

It was Amy's turn to bristle. "I suppose it's fair to say I didn't form an opinion of my own. I'd heard about what happened and believed what I heard."

"Do you feel any ill will toward Miss Hughes?" Emma asked.

"What?" Amy shook her head. "No. Why would I?"

"I'm aware you and Mr. Hughes have a social acquaintance," Emma said, drawing Max into the conversation. Both of her guests shifted uncomfortably in their seats.

"It wasn't much of a social acquaintance. We met for coffee once or twice last summer," Amy said dismissively. "Once we realized he was the father of one of my soon-to-be students we both thought it was best to leave it at a couple of cappuccinos."

"It was mutual?" Emma leaned forward slightly. "The decision not to see each other socially again."

"Yes," both Amy and Max replied in unison.

They shared a startled glance and then Amy shifted in her seat to rest her elbows on the table, peering directly at Emma. "Are you really Kayleigh's aunt?"

Emma gave a soft snort but declined to confirm or deny Kayleigh's spin. "As we mentioned, we found evidence indicating Kayleigh's social-media accounts had been compromised. We've also determined her laptop has been hacked, and whoever did it is savvy enough to run all of these processes through various types of spyware designed to mask the user's presence as well as their activity."

Amy Birch held her gaze as she processed this information. "O-o-o-oh," she whispered, drawing the word out several beats. It was barely more than a gasp, but it undercut the hum of conversation around them. "You think I had something to do with this."

"You have a relationship with the victim. You've had social interaction with the victim's father. It may or may not have gone the way you preferred, and I would assume you have the skills to run spyware, being an industry professional."

"I can't believe this," Amy muttered.

"I checked your NetwkIn profile. You worked for Syscom before leaving to teach at Capitol Academy," Emma said, unperturbed by the other woman's incredulity.

"I did."

"And what did you do for them?" Emma persisted.

She seemed to weigh the cost versus the benefit of answering the question, then sighed. "I developed and tested cyber-security software for most small-to-medium-size business models," Amy admitted with a challenging lift of one eyebrow.

"Then you know about various forms of malware. How to detect them, how they get into a system and what they could do once they get a foothold," Emma said flatly.

Amy straightened her shoulders and lifted her chin. "I do, but it doesn't mean I have." She shook her head, her lip curling. "I certainly don't wormhole my way into the social-media accounts of my students. I'm a trained IT professional, not a hacker," she said, infusing the last word with a healthy dose of disdain.

"I see." Emma tapped her pen against the pad, where she'd hardly made any notes. "I was a hacker who turned into an IT professional," she said almost conversationally.

"Scared straight?" the other woman asked with a sneer.

"Something like that." Emma flashed a humorless smile. "You can understand why we'd want to speak to you, though?"

"Yes, but why would I do this? What do I have to gain?" Amy asked stiffly.

When Emma cast a pointed glance in Max's direction, the other woman waved the insinuation off.

"Yes, I had coffee with her father once or twice months ago," she said dismissively, waving a hand in Max's direction. "But nothing came of it. If you've done any internet dating before, Agent Parker, you'll know it's not unusual. A woman has to kiss a lot of frogs to find her prince."

"I think I've been called a frog," Max said, speaking into his coffee cup as he raised it to take a drink.

"I am familiar with the process," Emma assured her.

"Then you know what I mean."

"Why did you leave a lucrative corporate job to take a teaching position?" Emma asked, cocking her head to the side.

"Have you ever worked in corporate IT, Special Agent Parker?"

"No." Emma shook her head. "I went directly from university into the police academy."

"Then you may not know the salaries in the corporate world can't always make up for the sacrifices one makes in their private life. I was tired of working sixty- and seventy-hour weeks. I was up to my eyeballs in code nearly every day. I took on project after project and couldn't see where it would ever end. I wasn't enjoying my life. I didn't have a life. So I made a choice."

"It isn't as if teachers at Capitol Academy aren't making a decent living," Max interjected. "They're paid well above what most public-school teachers make, though I will say it's still not nearly as much as any teacher ought to be paid."

Amy inclined her head. "I can't believe I heard a member of the school board saying so. Do your fellow board members know you feel this way?" she asked with a knowing smirk.

Emma shot Max a glance. He hadn't mentioned being on the school board. Now she understood why Kayleigh was being granted more leniency when it came to the bullying accusations. She made a note of it on her pad, but quickly steered the conversation back to the woman across from her.

"So you left your job at Syscom for better quality of life," she said with a nod of encouragement.

"And because I want this next generation of kids to be more tech-savvy." Amy fiddled with the lid on her to-go cup. "I was hoping to get some of the younger students in my classes so I could talk with them about digital security and social-media issues." She flashed a self-deprecating smile. "I wanted to catch them before they became so heavily invested in their phones, not really realizing I'd have to start with middle schoolers to make any real difference. Principal Blanton was the one who decided we should focus on eleventh and twelfth graders. He is of the belief they need to develop better skills before they go off to college."

"Don't most of the older kids have solid computer skills already?" Emma asked. She herself had been coding before she had a driver's license, but she knew most kids had other interests as teens.

"They do," Amy conceded. "Heck, there's an eleventh grader who is already monetizing the makeup tutorials she posts." She shrugged. "I've spoken to Dr. Blanton and we're reworking the curriculum."

Emma pursed her lips for a moment, unsure if she wanted to give voice to the thought niggling at her. In the end, she decided it would be irresponsible of her not to ask. "Do you think it's possible whoever is posting these things may have learned the skills necessary to spoof accounts in your classroom?"

Again, the teacher responded with a sad smile. "Can I say absolutely not? No. But I will readily admit most of my students are far savvier about social media than I am. I may know the technology powering the platforms, but they know how to manipulate it. They create, edit and boost two or three multimedia posts in the time it takes me to choose a GIF."

"Have you taken a closer look at any of the posts yourself?" The way the other woman lowered her gaze before answering told Emma everything she needed to know. She leaned in and lowered her voice. "You had to have noticed the posts about the other students were coming from a secondary account in Kayleigh's name."

Color rose high on the other woman's cheeks. When she looked up, she stared directly at Emma, studiously avoiding looking in Max's direction. "I did, but you know as well as I do many people maintain multiple social-media presences. I have no way of verifying which accounts are real or if someone is being impersonated."

"We've been tracking and cross-referencing all the students mentioned in posts related under Kayleigh's name."

"Then you know other accounts are popping up," Amy said, confirming Emma's suspicion this woman was also trying to crack her case.

"We do," Emma confirmed.

"And you believe the person who has hacked Kayleigh's accounts is also behind some of those?"

"It's a possibility," Emma hedged. Narrowing her eyes, she asked, "What do you think?"

Blowing out an exasperated breath, Amy checked the time on her smartwatch and inched her chair back enough for her to wriggle out of it. "What do I think? I think there's someone out there trying to get the valedictorian expelled weeks before graduation day, but I have no idea why. I also think you're not actually Kayleigh's aunt, and it's time for me to get to school."

Max stood, moving his chair aside to create a path for her. "Thanks for meeting us today," he said as she sidled past.

She paused and looked him straight in the eye. "I'm sorry this is happening. Sorry for you. Sorry for Kayleigh and the other kids. But I can assure you I have nothing to do with it. I hope you and the board will keep my cooperation in mind, as I'm sure this topic will be number one on the agenda for the next meeting."

Then she turned to give her full attention to Emma. "I will do whatever I can to aid your investigation. If I can help, please reach out to me directly."

Max reclaimed his chair, and the two of them sat quietly in the hubbub of the busy café. At last, Max tapped the side of his cup twice, then asked, "What do you think?"

"I think Amy Birch is not the person we're looking for," she answered, considering each word as if needing to confirm his gut instinct.

"She has the knowledge and the access," he countered.

"But no motive," Emma concluded. Smirking, she lifted her coffee in a toast. "Who'da thought a guy like you could strike out so thoroughly?"

He shrugged unselfconsciously and tipped his cup against

hers. "Can't win them all." He sighed. "Which means we're back to square one."

"Hardly," she said, affronted. "We're way beyond square one." Pushing her chair back, she rose. "Come on. I'll drop you off and head into the office."

# Chapter Ten

Max's ego was only slightly dented by Amy Birch's indifference to him. He may have felt miffed by it if Emma Parker hadn't seemed so pleased by the other woman's lack of interest. They rode back to the house in silence, Emma quiet and deep in thought as she made the short drive. When she signaled the turn into his driveway, he cleared his throat, intending to ask her how she planned to proceed, but the words died in his mouth.

"Oh. Oh, nuh-uh—" Emma jammed the brakes so hard his seat belt caught him and threw him back so hard his head slammed into the headrest. "Stay here," she ordered, shifting the car into Park and flinging the door open. "Hey!" she shouted. "Stop right there! Police!"

He spotted a hoodie-clad figure ducking into the trees that lined the opposite side of his house, then disappearing. Emma stopped at the edge of the concrete pad, staring down at the steep downhill slope. This time of year, it would be thick with new growth and underbrush. Ignoring her command, he scrambled from the car and sprinted over to stand beside her.

"Who was—" he asked, adrenaline making him breathless.

Her head whipped around. "I thought I told you to stay put."

"Did you get a look at them?" Max demanded.

"Pretty sure it was a kid. Can't say much beyond that." She turned back to survey his garage door.

Whoever their culprit was, he and Emma had interrupted them in midmessage. Rivulets of black spray paint ran from each letter scrawled across his garage door. Emma grabbed hold of a sapling and used it as a tether as she scrambled down the incline a few feet.

"What are you doing?" he demanded. "You can't chase them, it's too steep."

"I'm not chasing them," she said, sliding her hand down the thin trunk until she was able to squat and pick something up. She held a spray-paint can pinched gingerly between her thumb and middle finger. "Help me back up," she gasped as she straightened.

He leaned down and grasped her wrist. "Let go of the tree."

She looked up and met his eyes. "As long as you promise not to let go of me," she said, breathless.

"I have you."

She relinquished her hold on the tree and he dug in. He grunted with the effort of anchoring them both as she scrambled back onto the driveway. Once she was back on solid ground, she placed the can carefully on the concrete. "Don't touch."

"I won't," he promised. "You okay?"

"Yeah, it's…" She glanced back at the drop-off. "One heck of a slope. Kid must be part mountain goat."

"Or scared enough not to care," he said grimly.

Moving in unison, they turned back to the house. The message painted onto his once pristine white garage door glared back at them.

Their street artist only got as far as *LYING B* before being interrupted.

Emma pulled her phone from her pocket. "You go in and check on Kayleigh. I'll get the Little Rock police up here to take a report."

"The Little Rock police?" He shook his head. "You can't make the report?"

"Not my jurisdiction."

"Yeah, but—"

"Max," she said, interrupting his protest. "Go in and check on Kayleigh."

She spoke the order so firmly he had no choice but to obey. Turning on his heel, he ran for the front door. He had to punch in the code twice before the dead bolt released. The alarm panel flashed a red light, indicating video surveillance was activated. Moving to the panel, he punched in his six-digit code to disarm the alarm, then pulled his phone from his pocket. He could check the security footage on the app, and maybe get a look at the punk who did this.

"Kay?" Max called into the depths of the silent house. He thumbed open the security application as he rushed down the hall toward her bedroom. "Kayleigh, answer me," he called, his demand harsh with anxiety.

A heart-stopping beat passed before he heard a watery reply coming from the back of the house. "In here…"

Forgetting all about the camera footage, Max jogged down the hall to the primary suite, where he found Kayleigh sitting sideways on the teak bench situated inside the massive shower, her knees drawn up to her chin.

Slowing his steps, he approached with caution. "Hey, are you okay?"

His daughter didn't lift her head from the cradle of her arms. "Not a good question, Dad," she answered in a choked voice.

"I know," he conceded. "What happened? Did someone try to get in?"

"Yeah… No." She turned her head away from him, as if trying to block him out of her misery.

"What happened?"

She shook her head and gasped out another sob.

He patted her back, knowing the gesture was ineffectual,

but not knowing what else to do. "I'm kind of at a loss here, kid." He squatted down in front of the bench, grasping the edge to keep his balance. "I don't know what to ask you. I don't know what to say. I don't know how to handle any of this," he admitted quietly. "But I'm trying."

"I know," she whispered.

"There's no manual for being a parent," he said with a rueful smile. "I can't tell you how many times I've wished there was."

She sniffled deeply, then released a shuddering breath. "Maybe you should write one."

He scoffed. "I think we could both agree I'm hardly an expert."

"You do okay," she conceded huskily.

"Can you tell me what happened?" he asked her. She nodded without looking up. He gave her back a pat. "Come on. Sit up."

She took a deep breath before lifting her head and turning on the bench. Max pressed his hands to his aching knees and pushed up to his full height.

"Do you know who it was?" She nodded again.

"They spray-painted the garage door." Max wet his lips, uncertain of how much information he should share. "I'm gonna let you guess what kind of words."

"Oh, God," she moaned, then dropped her face into her hands again. "What did I ever do to him?"

"Do what to who, Kayleigh?" he asked gently. "Who did this?"

Kayleigh looked up, wiping her moist face with the insides of her wrists as she shook her head in despair. "Daddy, it was Carter," she said, her voice a croak. "He came and knocked on the door, but I didn't want to answer. I heard him drive off, but a few minutes later I heard something and looked out the window." She swiped at her eyes again, then looked up, her face a mask of misery. "He was out there yelling stuff. Mean stuff. Like we haven't known each other our whole lives. How could he do this?"

"Sweetie, I think everyone is feeling really, uh, raw right now," Max said carefully. "Didn't Emma say Carter was mentioned in some of those fake posts?"

"Yeah, but he *knows* me, Daddy," she wailed.

She searched his eyes for answers and he had none. There were no traces of the self-assured teenager he'd raised, or the young woman ready to take on the world.

"I don't know what to say," Max said, opting for honesty. "I don't have an answer for any of it, sugar. I wish I did, but I don't. All we can do is help Emma and the rest of her team collect whatever evidence they need to figure out who's doing this to all of you. Then maybe, once everyone sees the truth, we can all move on."

Kayleigh switched to the backs of her hands for the mopping up under her eyes. "Move on," she said with a bitter laugh.

"Listen, Emma's calling the Little Rock police in to take the report. He dropped the spray paint. I assume they'll be able to get fingerprints from it," Max informed her.

"I don't want Carter to get in trouble," she said, unfolding her long legs in preparation for leaping to her feet. "He has a scholarship from the Jones Foundation."

Max winced. Funded by a local family obsessed with their squeaky-clean, do-gooder image, the Jones Foundation awarded scholarships based on their own definition of good character and high standards.

"He probably should have thought about his scholarship before he vandalized somebody's property," Max said stiffly. "I'll to go see what's happening outside."

Kayleigh followed him. "Please don't press charges."

"I can't let him get away with this, Kayleigh."

"But you can. We can't… If you turn him in, it will look like we're picking on someone else," she said, a plea in her tone.

He turned back to her. "We haven't picked on anyone though, have we?" He fixed her with a stern glare.

"No. Of course not," she said, taken aback.

"I believe in the truth. The evidence Emma is tracing will exonerate you, and other evidence will prove Carter Pierce vandalized our home."

She shook her head hard and grabbed on to his sleeve. "You're concerned for my future but what about Carter's?"

He stilled, his grip on taking a hard line wavering. "Carter's parents can worry about his future."

"Hasn't there been enough damage done? Can't we let it be?" she asked, her voice rising with panic. "Can't we figure out who's doing all this, make it stop, and then everything can go back to the way it was?"

He turned and took her into his arms for a hard, fast hug. "Nothing's gonna go back to the way it was," he said. When she didn't pull away, he took the opportunity to press his cheek to the top of her head like he had when she was small. "But things can only get better, right?"

"Why do I feel like you've jinxed us?" she asked with a humorless laugh.

He gave her one last squeeze then turned toward the front door. "I'm gonna go talk to Emma and see if the police are here yet. I'll let her know it was Carter. Maybe she can find a way to talk to them without getting him in too much trouble."

"But you won't press charges?"

"I won't press charges," he promised, "but I will speak with his parents." He relinquished his hold on her and gave her a gentle push toward the media room. "Go find something to watch to take your mind off this. I'll handle things out here."

"You're not going to be able to protect me forever, you know," she said solemnly.

"No, but as long as I have breath in my body, I'm going to try," he vowed.

"So dramatic."

She rolled her eyes, but Max was serious. "Protecting you is my job. The only job that matters."

Emma gave him a tremulous smile and nodded before turning away. He watched as she padded down the hall. When she disappeared into the other room, he turned to head back outside.

When he pulled open the front door, he found Emma squatting beside the can of spray paint, taking photos of it from every conceivable angle.

"I should have done this before I touched it," she said without looking up from her task. "Taylor's gonna have my hide. Total rookie mistake. You can tell they sure don't let me loose on crime scenes often. I can't even remember the most basic principles," she grumbled to herself.

"You saw it and you acted," he said reassuringly. "Besides, we don't need to worry about getting fingerprints off the can. Kayleigh recognized our culprit."

The announcement captured her full attention. She looked up at him, her eyes wide. "She did? Is she okay? Did they try to get into the house?"

Her concern for his daughter touched him. "She's okay." He sighed and ran a hand through his hair. "It was Carter Pierce," he said flatly. "He's one of Kayleigh's classmates, and—"

"The boy she went to homecoming with. The football player."

"Yes."

"Our hacker was posting about him from one of the fake Kayleigh accounts."

Max shoved his hands deep in his pockets to hide the fact that they were balled into tight fists. Never in his life had he felt as impotent as a parent as he did this week. Not even when Kayleigh was a newborn and her mother so terribly sick.

"She doesn't want me to press charges against him," he informed her. "She's worried people are going to think we'll be seen as bullying him."

"Bullying," Emma said in an undertone. "Nothing but bullies around here."

The warning blip of a police siren made them both jump.

A squad car had pulled into the driveway and stopped behind Emma's still idling car.

Max gave his head a shake, then decided to make himself useful. "I'll pull your car up and turn it off."

Emma nodded and began shooting photos of the painted garage door with its drippy letters. "Great. Thanks."

Max made his way to her car. Settled in the driver's seat, he took a closer look at the interior of her vehicle. Several empty water bottles rolled loose on the back floorboard. The console was littered with gum wrappers, loose change, a collection of mismatched fast-food napkins and a twisted-up, frayed phone cable.

The detritus didn't shock him. He'd seen her pull articles of clothing out of her trunk—he assumed she spent much of her time on the go, but from her comments it sounded like she did most of her work either at home or in the office. She was living much as he had fresh out of college. But then marriage and a baby had forced at least a semblance of order on his life. He noted the many differences between his life and hers as he pulled the car forward and shut it off.

Leaning against the fender, he hung back as Emma greeted the officers and walked them through what they'd found when they pulled up. He watched as one of them dropped to one knee beside the paint can and pulled on a latex glove. One officer listened to Emma's description of where the can was discovered as he dropped the spray-paint can into a plastic evidence bag and stood up.

The three of them moved to the side of the driveway overlooking the slope. From their stances and the way they jostled one another, he assumed Emma was taking a ribbing for the way she'd handled crime-scene evidence. To his relief, she seemed unperturbed.

If anything, she seemed to regret having called the local police now they knew who the culprit was. Max had no doubt she was itching to dive back into her own investigation rather than answer their questions.

When the officers finally made their way over to him, it was merely to confirm his name and contact information. They made a few more notes as Emma took more photos of the damaged door, then took their leave with the promise they would be in touch.

Max strolled over to meet Emma as they climbed into the patrol car and backed out. "What did they think?"

She stared at the marred garage door, gnawing on her bottom lip. "Vandalism doesn't seem to impress them."

"They didn't need to talk to me?" he asked. "I thought in light of the other stuff—"

"I didn't tell them about the other stuff."

He raised an eyebrow. "Did you tell them you're Kayleigh's aunt?"

She shrugged. "I told them we were together when we pulled into the driveway. We saw someone spray-painting on the door, and you went in to check on your daughter as I pursued the suspect down the hillside, where I came upon the can."

She pinned him with a pointed stare and Max held her gaze and bit back the urge to chuckle. Who was he to judge if she wanted to rewrite history a bit?

"So what's the next step?"

"I'm going to talk to Kayleigh about Carter. The LRPD is going to go speak to him and his parents. You can press charges if you want," she said, raising an inquiring eyebrow.

"Criminal trespass, malicious intent to deface property, any number of things."

"But you don't think I should," he concluded, judging by her tone.

Again, she let one shoulder rise and fall before turning to face him. "I don't know many seventeen- or eighteen-year-old boys who would react any better to the things being said about him online."

"Kayleigh is hoping that if I don't press charges this whole thing will blow over and things can get back to normal."

Emma gave him a sad smile. "Oh, the optimism of youth."

"These kids," he said dryly.

"It won't ever get back to the way it was for them," Emma said, sobering instantly. "This week is going to be an inflection point for them. Everything in their young lives will be measured in before and after. For all of them. Patrice, Kayleigh, Carter and who knows how many more." Looking him in the eye, she said, "If we don't stop them, there could be others. So many others." Her mouth thinned into a grim line. "Even if they don't do anything else, it's going to get worse. They'll turn on one another. If they haven't already."

"For something none of them are actually responsible for."

"All the more reason not to make it any worse for Carter." She gestured to the garage door. "I am sure it won't cost much to have this repaired."

"Not nearly as much as it's going to cost him…them in so many other ways," Max agreed.

"We have a plan," she said as they walked back into the house.

Surprised, he eyed her warily. "We do? How did I miss making a plan?"

"Not you-and-me we, me and my team," she explained as she brushed past him. "Let me call the boss while you go check on Kayleigh."

"I've checked on Kayleigh," he countered, watching as she walked away.

"Check again," she called without breaking stride.

She walked through his house as if she lived there. As if she belonged there. Like she hadn't appeared on his doorstep mere days before. He tore his gaze away as she disappeared into Kayleigh's room. Seeing her so at ease in his home made him nervous, but in a disturbingly pleasant way.

He wondered if she was gathering her belongings. Would she still leave today? They'd had an intruder on the premises. Should he call Simon and ask him to ask her to stay? Should he ask her himself? Did Kayleigh want her to stick around?

The last question spurred him to action.

"Hey, Kay," he called out before entering the media room—it had been his habit from her early teens. In those days, it had felt like an alien had moved into their home, and the only way he could keep the peace was to be sure neither of them made any sudden movements.

She looked up when he entered the room. "Yeah?" she said, pointing the remote at the screen and freezing the image of a morning talk show.

"So I was thinking, and it's totally up to you," he began, knowing he sounded wishy-washy. "But given everything going on I was wondering if you feel more comfortable having Special Agent Parker here?"

His daughter quirked an eyebrow. "We're back to 'Special Agent Parker' now?"

"Fine. Are you more comfortable having Emma here?" he asked with blunt exasperation.

Kayleigh cocked her head as if pondering the question. "Do you mean because she's a cop, or because of the hacking stuff?"

"Either, I guess," he said with a shrug.

"To be honest, most of the time I forget she's with the police," she said as if the notion was tinged with absurdity. He was about to question her when she continued on. "I mean, she's so cool. I never really think of adults being so cool, and certainly not police officers," she said with a laugh.

Max clamped down on the indignity urging him to ask if his kid thought he was cool. Of course, she didn't. He stepped farther into the room. "You really think she's cool?" he asked. He couldn't help wondering what qualified Emma for a status he'd never achieve in his daughter's eyes. Was it merely because she was not a parental figure? Or was it because she was a whip-smart young woman doing a job most people would assign to nerdy guys?

"She's really chill, you know?" Kayleigh set aside the remote control when he perched on the far end of the couch. "Look how far she's come," she said admiringly. "You know, Emma told me she was bullied in high school. She said at first, she was really depressed and upset about it." She glanced down at her clasped hands and wet her lips. "I imagine she was probably a lot like Patrice. She was never the type to push back, you know?"

Max nodded. "She is pretty shy and reserved."

"But Emma said she eventually got so fed up with people trying to get one over on her it made her want to be smarter and faster. She didn't crumble," Kayleigh said in conclusion. "She stood up for herself."

Max thought about the sketchy information he'd gleaned about Emma's past. "Did she tell you what it was she did to make herself feel better?"

Kayleigh ducked her head, and he caught sight of the slight curl of her lips.

"She did, didn't she?"

"Not the details," Kayleigh assured him. "She only said she made it clear to the people who were giving her a hard time she was no pushover, but in the process, she got in trouble."

"Simon told me she was arrested when she was fifteen for hacking into her school's mainframe." Max eyed his daughter warily. "She was lucky her case landed with a judge who had some empathy for her situation."

"Oh, I knew about the arrest thing," Kayleigh said dismissively. "I was talking about the other thing."

Max raised an eyebrow. "What other thing?"

"I don't know if I should say," his daughter hedged. "I mean, if she hasn't told you, I don't know if it's my place to tell you."

"You're telling me she did something worse than figuring out how to alter school records? You know she changed the grades of the students who tormented her, right? She wasn't even old enough to drive a car legally," he pointed out.

"Well, yeah, it was worse, but not like, illegal or anything."

Max exhaled long and loud. "I think maybe you and I have two different definitions of what may be better or worse in this case."

"She's wondering if she should tell you I used to cut myself," Emma said, her tone flat and factual.

# Chapter Eleven

Max's and Kayleigh's heads swiveled. She knew she should have made her presence known, but listening to them talk about her had been too tempting. Once a wallflower, always a wallflower, she supposed.

Standing in the doorway, her laundry basket propped against one hip, she flailed her arm in a vain attempt to keep the collection of bags she'd hiked onto her shoulder from sliding.

Max jumped up to help relieve her of some of the burden. "I take this to mean you're leaving," he said as he lifted the straps from her arm.

When she freed herself of the last one, she caught him staring at the crosshatch of the thin silver-white scars on the inside of her forearm. "It was a phase. My mother saw what I was doing and got me the help I needed," she assured him.

"I'm sorry. It wasn't my intention to pry."

"No, I understand," she quickly assured him. "I don't try to hide them. The scars are a part of who I am." She flashed a wan smile. "I literally wouldn't be the woman I am today if I hadn't gone through something similar to what Kayleigh is navigating now."

"I hope you realize both Kayleigh and I are grateful for all you're doing. Having you here has been a big comfort to both of us." He glanced over at his daughter. "Hasn't it, Kayleigh?"

"Oh, yeah," Kayleigh said, swinging her legs down and sitting up straighter. "I mean, do you have to go?"

"There's really no reason for me to stay. We've pinpointed a point of access, and you know not to go anywhere near the laptop until we tell you it's clear, right?"

"Yes, ma'am." Kayleigh gave an exaggerated shudder. "Doubt I'll want to ever again."

"I'll get you a new one. I was going to upgrade you before you left in the fall, anyway," Max said.

Emma nodded her approval. "Good call. We may still need to use this one for the case. I need to think it through. Either way, leave it alone. Once we're done and it's released from evidence, I can wipe it so no one can get your information from it." She directed her next comment directly to Kayleigh. "If you need me, my apartment is only about ten minutes away, depending on traffic."

"But you're still going be working on the case, right?"

Emma tried not to read too much into how confused and somewhat panicked Max seemed to be by the notion of her leaving. He was nothing more than a concerned parent trying to swim in uncharted waters.

"Of course," she replied. "Why wouldn't I be?"

"Wouldn't it be easier for you to work on it here?" Kayleigh chimed in.

When Emma hesitated, Max lifted the heavy bags from her arm entirely. Emma sighed with relief as he set them aside.

"Kayleigh has a point. If you're going to keep monitoring her devices and checking her accounts, wouldn't it be easier to do it from here?" He reached for the laundry basket, and though she wanted to thrust it at him, she clung to it like a life raft. "Unless you need to be in the office—"

"I can work from anywhere."

"So this is as good a place as any." Max gave the basket a tug and she relinquished it without protest.

"You can have the guest room." Kayleigh twisted to kneel on the couch cushion, her eagerness disarming. "You won't have to worry about me barging in and getting stuff all the time."

"I wasn't worried about you barging in," Emma said with a laugh. "I was worried about being in your way."

"You aren't in my way," Max and Kayleigh said, speaking over one another.

She laughed again. "Most people would be happy to get their space back."

"Oh, I will be," Kayleigh said in a rush. "I mean, you know, because all my stuff is in there." The girl wrinkled her nose in an apologetic grimace.

"I totally get it," Emma said easily. "But there really is no particular reason for me to stay here. I can manage all your accounts from my apartment. You don't need to have me underfoot."

"What if we feel safer having our own special agent on the premises?" Max asked.

A hot flush of pleasure coursed through Emma. She curled her hand into a ball in an effort to contain her rising excitement. The truth was, she dreaded returning to a life of sub sandwiches eaten on the sofa.

"O-o-kay," Emma said slowly. "If you're sure I'm not in the way and—"

"You're not in the way," Max said without hesitation.

"Totally not," Kayleigh chimed in. "I like having someone other than my dad to talk, too." She shot Max a side-eye glance, but Emma was no longer fooled by the teen's bluster. She was as crazy about her father as he was her.

"Yeah, well, you're not the most scintillating conversationalist either, kid," Max retorted. Turning to Emma, he said, "I'll speak to Simon if you need me to clear it with him."

Emma huffed a laugh. "He's not my father."

"Yes. No. Right. I understand." He stumbled over his words,

and she loved knowing she had the power to fluster this ruth-lessly put-together man. "I meant in an official capacity."

"Tell you what." She nodded to the laundry basket of folded clothes he still held. "I'll leave my stuff here for now. I'm going into the office to meet with the team. We have a plan to isolate the computer we believe some of the posts were sent from. I also have some people analyzing social-media posts for trends. I'll touch base with the others and brainstorm next steps."

"But you're going to come back here," Kayleigh persisted.

Emma shrugged, then gestured to the bags and basket. "I'll have to at least come by. You have most of my stuff."

"If this is most of your stuff, we're going to have to have a serious talk about your skin-care regimen," Kayleigh mut-tered, falling back into the seat again.

Emma only smiled as she turned to Max. "I think maybe it's time for you to reach out to the other parents. I'm sure by now at least some people have started figuring out there's something more complex going on here."

"I tried to reach out to Patrice's parents, but they haven't returned any of my calls," Max informed her.

She sighed. "I'm betting Carter Pierce's parents are going to take your call." Emma glanced at her watch. "Give them about an hour, then give them a try."

She bent over and pulled Kayleigh's phone from her mes-senger bag. Kayleigh's face brightened, but Max eyed the de-vice warily.

"I'm leaving this with your dad. I don't want you using it to call your friends, even if your pal Tia has called twenty-seven times. And I definitely want you to stay off social media." She handed the device over to Max. "But I do not want you left alone without some form of communication again. So this is for dialing nine-one-one only. You get me?"

Kayleigh nodded, her expression sober. "I get you."

"When I get back, you and I will talk about reaching out

to some of your friends to see if we can get a line on the general feelings out there and where we stand."

Kayleigh wrinkled her nose, but this time in distaste. "I don't know if I want to talk to anybody," she admitted.

"I get it." Emma flashed her a weak smile but gestured to the phone again. "But I think it would be a good strategic move. People will understand why you were incommunicado for a day or two. Most people would assume your dad has your phone and you've been cut off from all other electronics."

"Then they would assume correctly," Kayleigh said with no lack of sarcasm.

"But it's about time for us to make it look like you're sneaking around the blockade," she said with a sly smile.

"I'm not so sure I like the sound of this," Max admitted.

"What kid wouldn't take the first opportunity they had to break the embargo?" Emma asked.

"This is the part in the movie where the teenagers make the parents look like clueless idiots."

Emma laughed as she picked up her messenger bag again and left the rest of the pile at his feet. "Don't flatter yourself. The parents in those movies look like clueless idiots from the jump," she said with a smirk. "I'll be back soon. Call me if you need me."

SIMON PRESSED THE tips of his fingers into the scarred top of the conference table and they all quieted. "Tell me what you've got," he ordered as he took his seat.

Emma and Wyatt exchanged a look, as always slightly taken aback by their boss's obvious distaste for small talk. At the far end of the table, the two newest members of the Cyber Crime Division, agents Caitlin Ross and Tom Vance, looked like they would rather be anywhere else.

"If you don't mind, I'd like to listen to what everybody else has been working on first," Emma said briskly. "I have some thoughts I'm trying to put together, but I need to know if I'm missing any puzzle pieces."

Simon inclined his head. "Dawson, kick things off."

Beside her, Wyatt sat up straighter in his chair. "I've been talking with Emma and I think we're on the same page as far as the Information Technology teacher is concerned," he began. "If she were our perp, I think she'd have done a better job of masking things."

"Their tracks were covered pretty well," Simon said without hesitation.

"Pretty well," Wyatt conceded, "but well enough for a person who spent years designing security software?" He shook his head. "I don't think so."

"You're saying you think she's too good to be our hacker," the section chief concluded.

Emma and Wyatt shared a look, and then Emma spoke up. "Yes. I think she has enough experience in the field of cybersecurity to have made it much tougher on us. We know the tools we're working with aren't anywhere near the cutting edge, and up until eighteen months ago she was in the thick of it with this Syscom. If she was behind all this, I'd have to think she'd have known of a better way."

Simon gave a curt nod. "Concur."

"Aside from her experience in the field, my gut instinct when I met her was she was not our mark."

"Good enough," Simon said briskly. "Moving on."

The two newer members of their team, Tom and Caitlin, shared a look of disbelief at their end of the table.

When all eyes swiveled in their direction, Tom shifted in his seat uncomfortably. Knowing what it was like to be caught in the glare of Simon Taylor's unrelenting stare, Emma lobbed them a softball. "You find any correlations in the social-media posts?"

Caitlin responded, "I have a short list of names of people

you may want to discuss with Miss Hughes. The one I'm most curious about is Tia Severin."

"Tia Severin? Why?"

Caitlin glanced over at Tom before answering. She looked distinctly uncomfortable. "I don't have any hard data. Something in my gut tells me her responses to some of the things being said about her best friend and their classmates comes across as…disingenuous?"

"We don't discount gut instincts in this room," Simon said without looking up from his notepad. "Data is king, but it's not an absolute ruler. We all know it can lie as easily as a human being controlling it."

"If you would send me a compilation of the posts you think I need to go over and flag anything of particular interest to you, I would appreciate it," Emma told the younger agent.

Caitlin straightened her shoulders, a pink flush staining her cheeks. "Sure. I've already made a ton of notes, but I'd be happy to go over them with you. Maybe things will strike you differently from how they struck me."

Emma nodded. "We'll get together after this meeting."

She turned to Wyatt. "Did you have any chance to think any further on replacing the computer tower in the IT lab?"

Simon looked up. "Good idea to swap it for one we can monitor from here."

"I'll call Amy Birch to see if they have an extra CPU of the same brand not currently in use," Wyatt said, making a note on his pad.

"Are you sure you want to tip the teacher off?" Simon asked.

Emma and Wyatt exchanged a glance and he nodded. "We don't think she's our hacker."

"Fine." Simon made a mark on his notepad. "You two work on the CPU. Ideally, I'd like to get it set up so we can make the swap when no one else is around."

"Sounds good," Emma agreed. "I think we can get Amy Birch's help with arranging the swap."

Simon flipped the cover on his notebook and clicked his pen decisively. "Okay, we know where we're at now." He pushed his chair back from the table and stood. "Parker, I want you to stick close to the Hughes house. I don't like the thought that some kid was prowling around when his daughter was home alone."

"Yes, sir."

"As a matter of fact, I think I want you to take a patrol car."

Emma gaped at him. She hadn't ridden in a patrol car in years. "Sir?"

"We don't want any more of his friends coming around." He paused in the doorway and turned back to her. "I think it would be good to have a marked car in the driveway."

"Respectfully, I disagree," Emma said, coming to her feet. "Sir."

Simon froze for a second then zeroed in on her, one eyebrow lifting. "Oh?"

"Not yet, at least." Emma glanced at Wyatt for backup, and he nodded his agreement. "We're still gathering information, and as far as we know the only person who's aware we're involved aside from Dr. Blanton is Amy Birch. The last thing I want to do is tip people off to our presence."

Seconds seemed to tick by at a glacial pace as she waited for her boss to weigh his options. At last, Simon gave a nod and clicked his pen twice, a clear mark of concession. "You're lead on this, Parker, so you make the call."

"Thank you, sir," Emma said, anxious to call close to the meeting before he could change his mind.

Wyatt and Tom gathered their belongings and followed the boss out. The moment the men cleared the room Caitlin let out a weary breath. "He doesn't say much, but you don't really have to read between the lines with him, do you?" she asked.

Emma grinned, tickled by the other agent's assessment of their boss. "It's what I like best about him. A person always knows exactly where they stand with Simon Taylor."

She kicked back in the chair and tipped her chin up as she stared at the water-stained ceiling tiles.

"I want to echo what Simon said about not ignoring your gut instincts. If you have a feeling about something, I want you to share it with me."

"Yes, ma'am."

"And it's Emma, not ma'am," she said, shooting the other woman a sidelong glance. "So tell me, what's your gut saying?"

There was a long pause and then Caitlin replied, "I agree with you. The kids are talking. There's a lot of back-and-forth, and all the usual ugliness," she said with a sharp laugh. "But there's a kind of malicious intent behind the posts being made by Kayleigh's accounts. It seems more…mature." She winced. "Not the right word, but the best one I have at the moment."

"I get you." Emma nodded, her gaze fixed on a water mark. It looked sort of like a lion's head. "I know exactly what you mean. Whoever it is, they're an adult familiar enough with the language kids use with one another to be able to mimic it, but there's something stiff in the delivery. Is *stilted* a good word?"

"Yes. Exactly," Caitlin replied, excitement rising. "Like I said, the kid who's really throwing up any flags for me is Tia Severin. It looks like up until last week she and Kayleigh were tight. Every other post on both of their feeds is tagged with each other, and every group photo, if one was in a group photo then the other was there, too." Caitlin leaned forward.

Emma lowered her gaze to give the other woman her full attention. "And what's irking you about what she's saying?"

"More what she isn't saying. She never comes to Kayleigh's defense, or even told Kayleigh to stop. But she also never egged her on like some of the other kids did." Caitlin shook her head. "Her posts were oddly…neutral."

"Hmm."

"She took almost no stance on the entire situation. Not only on the posts Kayleigh supposedly made about Patrice, but on all the subsequent posts from the spoofed account. It's like she couldn't resist commenting, but she had nothing to add to the conversation. She wasn't supporting anyone, nor was she dragging them. She reminds me of a politician walking the line on a touchy issue."

Emma stared at the younger agent, impressed with the assessment.

Scooting forward in her chair, she slapped an open palm to the tabletop as she rose. "You've got me intrigued. Grab your notes and we'll make an attempt to decipher the coded messages of adolescents. You wanna hang out at your cubicle or mine, Agent Ross?"

THE COMPUTERS USED in the Capitol Academy information-technology lab were a common model. Wyatt was able to unearth one from the boneyard of outdated and confiscated hardware they kept locked in an evidence cage. They had it loaded with all the software Amy Birch listed for them and ready to go by midafternoon, but the teacher insisted they wait until 5:00 p.m. to deliver it, to be sure no one but Ms. Birch was still at the school.

At 4:45 p.m., they watched from a parking lot across the street as a man wearing a whistle around his neck exited the building with a mesh bag of soccer balls. The wipers swished away a fine mist of rain. Emma squinted at the guy as he moved to one of the two cars left in the staff parking lot and tossed the bag of balls into the back seat before climbing in.

"You do a lot of extracurriculars in school?" Wyatt asked, not taking his eyes off the man.

Emma scoffed. "Hardly."

"You keep trying to make me believe you've been cool your whole life, but there's too much nerd in you," he said, elbowing her across the console.

"It wasn't a matter of being cool. It was more I've never been a great team player," she said, watching as the car turned right out of the parking lot.

"You are, too," he countered.

"Now I am," she admitted as he started the engine of the state-issued SUV. "I bet you were on all the teams."

Wyatt nodded as he put the car into Drive. "Of course, I was. When you grow up in a town the size of a postage stamp, you need every warm body you can scrape together to even make a team."

"I bet you were the star player," she teased.

"Hardly," he said with a chuckle. "I did okay with baseball, though."

"Of course, you did—you're the all-American boy," she joked, mimicking his tone.

Wyatt cruised across the street and into a spot beside the lone vehicle left in the staff lot. It was a late-model crossover with a bumper proclaiming every inch of distance its owner had conquered.

Emma gave it the side-eye as they pulled in. "I'll never understand people who run marathons for fun."

Wyatt killed the engine. "I thought you were a runner," he said with a puzzled frown.

"I ran to keep in shape, not to collect those obnoxious medals they hand out. Some of them are the size of dinner plates."

"Maybe if you had a couple of those dinner-plate medals, you wouldn't have to eat off wrappers every night."

"Har, har," she said as she reached for the door handle.

"Maybe they aren't in it for the medals. Maybe they're chasing the high. Or it was nothing more than a goal they wanted to achieve," he said, raising a single eyebrow in challenge.

"Then shouldn't the achievement be reward enough? Does the whole world need to know about it?"

"You're a sour case, Emma Parker, but something about this lady gets under your skin," he teased with a grin. "Wouldn't have anything to do with the online dating thing she had with Mr. Huge-bucks, would it?"

Emma shuddered "Please don't call him that. The creepers online are always referring to him by that name and it's weird. He's a nice guy. He has a nice house, and a nice car. I can only assume he makes a good living, but I have never asked. Regardless, it doesn't mean he or his daughter—"

Wyatt reached over and gave her a friendly pat. "Easy, Em. I was only joking around."

She swatted his hand away and flipped the hood on her windbreaker up to cover her head. "Let's get this over with."

"You got someplace better to be?" he asked as he opened his door. "Oh, right, you do."

"Anywhere away from you would be better, Dawson," she muttered, following him out of the car.

The two of them hurried across the lot, dodging puddles leftover from an afternoon rain shower. She followed Wyatt up the steps, her attention drawn to the mini CPU he said matched the units used by the school. Even the secondhand computers donated to Capitol Academy were better than most. No big, bulky towers taking up room underneath the desks for their computer lab.

"I always hated being the last person at school," Wyatt said as they approached the main doors. "So creepy."

Emma nodded. "Like a scene from one of those teen slasher movies," she said, wrinkling her nose.

Wyatt tried the handle on the door to the far right as Amy Birch had instructed, but found it was locked. He tried the other two before coming back to the one on the right. The soccer coach had exited through it only minutes before.

Emma frowned at the transom windows above the doors. There were still lights on inside, but they were clearly not at full power. Had the custodian come around and locked it already?

"I thought she said the custodian didn't lock the school until five thirty or six?" Emma went down the line, testing each door as if she hadn't watched Wyatt try them all. Not a single handle gave way.

"That's what she told me."

Emma glanced back at the parking lot. "I'd bet dollars to doughnuts she drives the marathon car. Try calling her."

Wyatt handed off the computer and pulled his phone from his back pocket. Misty drops of rain gathered on the screen as he placed the call and switched it to speaker. It rang four times before Amy Birch's chirpy voice invited them to leave a message.

"Hey, Ms. Birch, Wyatt Dawson here. We're outside, but the doors are locked. It looks like you're still in the building. When you get a chance if you could come let us in, I promise we'll be in and out quick as a flash." He held Emma's stare for a beat, then disconnected.

Holding the computer close to her chest, Emma walked back down the steps and crossed the lawn, the rubber soles of her shoes squeaking on the wet grass. She peered around the corner of the building to the lane reserved for school-bus loading. There was an older-model compact car with a dented fender and rust spots showing through its dull gray paint parked in the lane.

"Maybe that's the custodian, parked in the bus lane?" she called as she made her way back to the entrance.

Wyatt nodded. "We'll give it a minute, and then I'll pound on the door and see if we can get someone's attention."

Emma nodded and took a moment to survey the manicured grounds of the city's most exclusive private high school. The other end of the building was flanked by the best athletic fields money could buy. The planters on either side of the carved wooden doors were brimming with freshly planted seasonal flowers. They wouldn't have lasted a day at her old school.

"Can you imagine going to a school like this?" she asked.

Beside her, Wyatt shook his head. "I'm glad I didn't. Too much competition over things that don't really matter," he said gruffly.

"No doubt," Emma concurred. "The things Kayleigh tells me." She shook her head. "All I can say is you couldn't pay me to be a teenager again."

"Amen," Wyatt said, wiping mist from his face. "Okay, time to start pounding."

He turned back to the door and gave it a series of hard thumps with the side of his fist. As they waited for a response, he checked his phone again. He gave his head a shake before shoving it back into his jeans pocket.

"You want me hold it?" he asked, gesturing to the computer.

Emma looked down at the computer. It was no bigger than a hardback novel and certainly lighter. "You think I can't hold on to this monster of a machine?"

"Nothing to do with capabilities, Parker," he said, shaking his head in slow exasperation. "You know my mama raised me to be polite."

"Oh, I know. I've got it," she assured him, then slid the computer inside her windbreaker to protect it from the damp weather.

Wyatt walked back down the steps and tramped through the grass to the side of the building.

"The car is still parked there," he said as he stomped back up the steps. "We should have come earlier."

"We couldn't risk anybody else seeing us. Only Ms. Birch

and Dr. Blanton know we suspect anything more than a social-media spat."

Wyatt came back up to the doors, raised both fists and pounded on the center one for a full thirty seconds. Emma winced with each reverberating thud.

He was lowering his arms when they heard the *thunk* of the crash bar on the other side. The door flew open, sending them scurrying back to avoid being struck.

A tall, bald man in work pants and a shirt identifying him as Chuck appeared in the doorway, breathless and frantic. "Are you the police?"

Emma and Wyatt exchanged a confused glance before she stepped forward and said, "Yes. I'm Special Agent Emma Parker, Arkansas State Police. This is Agent Dawson."

The man's brow wrinkled. "The state police? Is the ambulance coming?" he asked, peering past them, breathless.

"Ambulance?" Emma looked down and saw the man had damp spots of blood on his pants leg and a smear on his hand. She stepped into his space. "Has something happened?"

"I dialed nine-one-one," he said, nodding so hard Emma was afraid he'd give himself whiplash. He craned his neck to look beyond them. "It's taking too long."

In the distance, Emma heard the wail of a siren approaching.

"We were here to meet Ms. Birch," Wyatt informed him. "What's going on?"

"Ms. Birch?" he said, his eyes darting between them.

"Yes," Wyatt confirmed. "Is she here?"

"She's the reason I called nine-one-one," Chuck explained. "I found her in the computer room. She's bleeding. And unconscious."

Emma dropped the computer and it hit the concrete steps with a sharp crack. Without waiting, she and Wyatt pushed past the other man.

"Which way?" Emma asked the custodian.

"Down the hall, take a right, third door on the left," he called back. "But wait—"

"You stay there," she ordered, turning back as Wyatt sprinted ahead. "Let the paramedics know where we are. Tell the local police what you found."

Confused, Chuck gestured to the now broken computer unit at his feet. "But what about this?"

Unwilling to be delayed a second longer, Emma shook her head and shouted, "It's trash now," then took off at a dead run.

## *Chapter Twelve*

It was well past the dinner hour by the time Emma pulled into Max Hughes's driveway. Though it was still daylight, golden light spilled from expansive glass windows. She sat in her car for a moment, taking in the beautiful house with its perfectly maintained flower beds and precisely clipped lawn.

A coat of white paint had been applied to the garage door but was proving insufficient when it came to covering up the spray paint. No doubt, Max had made the attempt to erase the ugliness so Kayleigh didn't have to look at it.

She got out of her car and walked over to the garage to examine the not-so-perfect door.

The slapdash cover-up was clearly a temporary solution. She wouldn't be at all surprised if she woke the next day to find a professional house-painting crew hard at work restoring the door to its former glory.

But she understood why he couldn't let it stand as it was for the night. She moved back a few steps and tilted her head to the right, squinting at the faint outline of the large capital *B*.

The front door opened, and Max stepped outside dressed in a pristine white T-shirt and black joggers. His feet were bare, and his hair was damp.

"Hey," he called out to her. "I was wondering when you'd be back."

"Hey," she replied. She ran a hand through her hair. "Sorry, it's been a doozy of a day." Gesturing to the door, she asked, "I'm assuming this was you?"

"I cleared it with the LRPD first," he assured her, sounding only slightly defensive.

"Did you tell them you're not pressing charges against Carter Pierce?"

He nodded. "I did. I also spoke to Carter and his parents this afternoon. He offered to come over and paint the door himself, but I figured Kayleigh wouldn't want him around."

"Probably not." She crossed her arms over her chest and rocked back on her heels. "I bet his folks were grateful. Did you explain to them what has been happening?"

He shook his head. "I didn't go into detail because I didn't know what you would want me to say or keep quiet, but I let them know Kayleigh was not responsible for the posts on her accounts."

"Probably all they needed to hear for now," she said with a judicious frown. "Did you talk to anyone else?"

He nodded. "Patrice's mother finally returned my call."

"And?"

"They are doing okay. Patrice will make a full recovery and has started seeing a therapist." He blew out a breath. "She wanted to talk to Kayleigh."

"Did you let them?"

"Yeah." He thrust his hands into his pants pockets. "We agreed they could talk on speaker and with her mom and me in the room."

"How'd it go?"

He let his head fall back, gazing up into the deepening twilight. "It was…heartbreaking for everyone, but I think good for them?" Shaking his head, he murmured, "So much pain. And for what reason? Who's getting something out of all this?"

He turned to look at her and she could only shrug. "Max,

I have to tell you, Amy Birch was attacked at the school this afternoon."

"What?" Max shook his head hard. "When? How? Why haven't I heard anything about this?"

She gave a tremulous smile. "Dr. Blanton is still speaking with the Little Rock police. I assume he'll call the school-board members and give you all an update soon."

"Is she badly hurt?"

Emma shook her head. "Someone gave her one heck of a whack on the head. She has a concussion. And the blow opened a small cut. It bled badly and scared the wits out of poor Mr. Johnson, the custodian."

"Who else was in the building?" he demanded.

"We're still gathering information, but I can tell you the soccer coach and Mr. Johnson were both on the premises in the timeframe."

"Was Blanton there? I know he usually stays late," Max said with a frown.

She shook her head. "He was not. Mr. Johnson said the administrative offices were empty, and when the LRPD reached out to him, he said he was coming from a dinner meeting."

Max rubbed his lips together as he digested this information. "And she was attacked in her classroom?"

Emma shook her head. "In the computer lab."

"Any idea what they hit her with?"

"We're not one-hundred-percent positive, but our best guess at this juncture was it was a computer."

"A computer? Like a laptop?" he asked, puzzled.

But Emma could only continue to wag her head. "No. A desktop CPU," she informed him grimly. "We found bits of the plastic casing near where Ms. Birch lay, and fragments in her hair."

"Has she regained consciousness?" Max asked, concern etched into every line of his handsome face.

"Yes. The paramedics were able to bring her around. She didn't know anyone but Mr. Johnson was in the building."

Max shook his head in disbelief. "Someone hit her with a computer?"

"Not any old computer, but *the* computer."

"The computer?" he echoed.

"We checked the serial numbers of the units left behind and none matched the one we suspected our hacker was using. We were going in to swap it out with a dummy, but now it's gone."

"It's gone."

Emma hooked a hand through his arm and pointed him in the direction of the door. "You're turning into a parrot. Let's go inside."

"I can't believe someone attacked her. In the school," he added, his voice rising. "I need to call Dr. Blanton."

"Not yet," she said, propelling him to the entrance. "I need to talk with Kayleigh."

"She's in her room," he answered, falling into step beside her. "Does this mean you're going to stay?"

Her heart quickened at the hopeful note in his question. She tried not to read too much into it. Going for nonchalance she didn't feel, she said, "Simon says stick close." But it came out sounding flippant, and she saw a cloud darken Max's hopeful expression. Instantly contrite, she tried again. "Yes, I'm going to stay. If you still want me to."

"I put your things in the guest room. Kayleigh is right—you should be more comfortable there."

"Thank you." She ducked her head to hide her smile when he gestured for her to precede him through the door. "She's probably right about my skin-care regimen, too." He stopped walking so abruptly, so she drew up, too. "What?"

"You tell me," he countered. "Is there anything else I need to know? Has your team uncovered anything else?"

She shrugged. "We mostly went over technical details

for swapping the computers, but there's no point now." She pressed her lips together as she pondered how much to share with him. "One of the team has been monitoring posts other students make on social media. I'm going to talk to Kayleigh about a few of them, get her take on their personalities." She met his eyes. "We're all pretty sure it's an adult behind everything, particularly after what happened this afternoon, but have no solid evidence to back it up. A student could have snuck back into the school. It could have been another teacher, a coach, a parent..."

"So basically, we wait until something happens."

She tilted her head and gave him a wan smile. "Something has happened, Max. It's simply not the big breakthrough we all want. But we're putting pieces together. Sometimes figuring out who to look at is more about ruling people out."

"But doesn't provide solid evidence," he argued.

"We figure out who to look at, then we go looking for the evidence," she said in her most reassuring tone. "We're making progress. As we computer jockeys say, it takes a lot of bits to make a byte." She waved an arm toward Kayleigh's room. "Do you want to sit in? You might know some of the parents."

He chuckled mirthlessly, then shook his head. "I'd wager I know most of the parents, but no. You talk to Kayleigh, and if there's something the two of you think I should look at, let me know. I don't want to trample her voice in all this."

"Good call," she said approvingly. "I think in a weird way, this could turn out to be a good thing for Kayleigh. She's growing. Learning to look at things from someone else's point of view, getting a good lesson on the ripple effect words and actions can have. It will shape her choices from here on out, and from what I've seen so far, I'd say likely for the better."

"Like it did for you?" His eyes widened and he pressed his knuckle to his mouth as if to stop anything else from escaping.

He looked so shocked by the sound of his own voice, she had to laugh. Giving his arm a friendly pat, she moved past him. "Exactly."

EMMA KICKED HER shoes off and shifted her weight so she could brace one foot on the rail of Kayleigh's bed frame, but she didn't reach out to touch the girl. Reading through days' worth of social-media vitriol had left Kayleigh crying into the pastel-blue tufted throw pillow she'd held clutched to her belly for most of their conversation. She waited until Kayleigh's sobs slowed to hiccups, then spoke.

"You know most of this is all talk, don't you?" Emma asked in a voice barely above a whisper. "Everyone is scared. Everyone is pointing fingers. Not only at you, but at each other. This is the kind of chaos these creeps live for."

"I hate this," Kayleigh said, snuffling. "This is supposed to be the best time of my life, and it's not. It sucks!"

"Oh, honey, any age ending with the word *teen* is not even in contention for the best time of your life." She sighed. "This next phase...the one where you start figuring out how to live someplace other than your parents' house, and how to make twenty dollars stretch to a week's worth of food." Kayleigh's expression of blank horror made her laugh. "Okay, you probably won't have to worry about your food budget, but life beyond high school is totally different."

"Well, yeah. I sure hope so," Kayleigh said, the petulance in her tone a stark reminder of how young and insulated she was.

"You'll start picking your friends from a wider pool. People from all over the world. They'll have different clothes, and new ideas, and your world view will expand. Sure, some will be jerks, but you'll also learn to sniff them out pretty quickly." She tapped the laptop and shot her a commiserating stare. "You never outgrow the haters, but you learn not to give them a parking space, you know?"

She tapped her temple and Kayleigh nodded. "Right."

Emma gestured to her laptop, open on the bed, then the room in general. "This was all a ramp-up. And how you handle this will be a good indicator of how you handle the other stuff life throws at you." She paused then dropped her voice. "You control the narrative."

"Unless someone clones your accounts and steals your voice," Kayleigh countered.

"You still have a voice," Emma insisted. "Sure, we've been quiet for a few days while we sort some stuff out and make sure other people are okay, but this is a strategic retreat. You will get the last word. I promise you." She stared intently into the young woman's eyes. "Do you believe me?"

Kayleigh began to nod before she answered. "Yes."

She pulled the sheaf of printouts she and Caitlin had made of some of the more questionable posts from her bag and placed them on the bed. "Now, tell me about Tia Severin."

"Tia?" Kayleigh asked.

"Yes." Emma waited, watching as Kayleigh drew back as if she'd dumped a bag of snakes onto the duvet. "Do you want to see some of the things she's been posting?"

Kayleigh narrowed her eyes. "Do I?"

Emma nudged the pile of papers. "There's nothing bad here. But she didn't come rushing to your defense, either," she said, raising a single eyebrow. "Tell me about your relationship with her. She's your best friend, right?"

"We've spent a lot of time together these last couple years," Kayleigh answered with admirable caution.

"How did you become friends?"

"The usual way." The younger woman shrugged. "We had a few classes together. We started hanging out more last year, I guess. She and her parents went to Europe the summer before eleventh grade. They were over there for about seven weeks during the summer, and I was so jealous."

"They were vacationing over there?"

"I think her dad had to work some, but yeah." She frowned as she thought back. "I remember going home and asking my dad why we couldn't go, too. After all, my dad owned part of Mr. Severin's company, so it totally would have made sense for us to go, too."

Emma reared back. "Your dad owned the company Mr. Severin worked for?"

"Not owned," she amended. "You know, he invested money in it to get it going."

"As part of his venture-capital investing," Emma said to confirm.

"Yeah. I didn't understand why we couldn't have gone, too. I would have loved to go to Milan. You should have seen some of the shoes Tia had."

"You guys bonded over shoes?" Emma asked as she slowly shuffled through the printouts looking for one message in particular.

"We both really like fashion in general," Kayleigh said. "Tia totally wanted to be a model, but seriously, if it hasn't happened by now... I mean she'll be eighteen next month. She's too old to be a model."

Emma sucked air in between her teeth, but refrained from commenting on Kayleigh's hot takes on aging.

"You said the two of you would take pictures of one another to post to Foto. Has she done any modeling locally?"

"She did a thing for a couple of department stores and a TV spot for a car dealer. It was so cheesy," she said with a laugh.

"But Tia's parents won't allow her to pursue modeling seriously?"

Kayleigh shook her head. "She isn't tall enough to be a fashion model. It's one of those things girls talk about, you know?"

"I see."

"Anyhow, CA is a supercompetitive school, and Tia is really, really smart. I mean, like, top-of-the-class smart," she said with a wave of her hand. "The girl got into Brown."

Emma looked up from the papers. "She's going to Brown?"

Kayleigh bit her bottom lip then grimaced as she shook her head. "No. Actually, she's going to stay in state, but she got into Brown," she explained with a sage nod. "There was some something about money and her dad's business." She waved her hand dismissively. "I don't know the details, but I'm sure my dad could tell you. Anyway, she's heading up to Fayetteville in the fall."

"Do most of the students at your school go out of state for college?" Emma asked, truly curious.

"I'd say it's about half and half. A bunch go up to the U of A, some to private schools around here. A couple guys got football scholarships from the University of Central Arkansas, but a good chunk go out of state."

"And for those who go out of state, I assume it's a decent percentage headed to the Ivies," Emma said as she found the post she'd been looking for. "Trading an acceptance at Brown for the U of A had to be a tough decision."

"I guess." Kayleigh shrugged. "Tia has always been a big mama's girl, though. Frankly I couldn't see her packing up her stuff and heading off to Providence."

"But you won't have any trouble packing up and going to Cambridge?" Emma asked.

Kayleigh looked up as if torn between rolling her eyes and trying not to cry. "Sure I will," she said softly. "But I think maybe it's probably the best thing for both me and my dad."

"How do you figure?"

"He and my mom got married really young. Like right-out-of-college young. And they had me right away. He's never really had a life on his own." She gave a chuckle. "He's going to be forty soon, so I guess it's about time."

"I have a feeling he'll be in the Boston area a lot more often than you think," Emma said dryly.

A slow, pleased smile spread across Kayleigh's lips. "Yeah. I know. It's okay."

Emma held up the sheet she was looking for and said, "Tia posted to ChitChat about how she was shocked you would say such horrible things to Patrice, but claims you have always had trouble distinguishing…" She consulted the paper she held. "Something authentic from a good knockoff."

Lowering the page, she looked Kayleigh straight in the eye. "What does she mean?"

"Are you kidding me?" Color rose high in Kayleigh's cheeks and she clamped her lips into a thin, angry line. Emma waited patiently as the girl drew calming breaths through flaring nostrils. "I wish she'd get over it already," she muttered.

"Get over what?"

"You know when I said her family went to Europe? Well, when she came back, she was carrying this supercute backpack bag with the Prada emblem on it, but it wasn't a real Prada bag," she said with a sympathetic wince. "I thought she knew. I made some comment about what good knockoffs people could find overseas, and she got all bent out of shape about it."

"Because you said her backpack was fake?"

Kayleigh rolled her eyes. "She kept insisting it was an authentic Prada, but anyone who knew anything could see it wasn't. The stitching was all wrong and the lining was awful. Anyway, she swore up and down it was the real deal. I know for a fact it wasn't, but I let it go because I wasn't the one walking around with the fake backpack, she was," she said in a rush of indignation.

"I guess she's hung on to at least some of her anger over it," Emma said, quietly passing the printout across to her.

Kayleigh looked down at the screen capture they'd printed.

"I guess so." She gave a short, sharp laugh then tossed the page aside. "She didn't hang on to her fake Prada backpack long," she said with an edge of snark. "I never saw it again."

"But y'all stayed friends."

"Yes."

"If you had to choose a label, would you say you were besties or frenemies?" Emma asked, genuinely curious.

"I'd say our relationship status is more like...best frenemies."

"Way to split the atom," Emma said dryly.

"Ask a simple question, get a complicated answer," Kayleigh retorted.

"Do you think she resents you?"

Kayleigh looked truly perplexed by the notion. "Resents me? For what?"

"Pick a reason," Emma replied. "You're about to be valedictorian. Off to Harvard. Your father's financial setbacks haven't directly impacted your future," she said, ticking off each option on her fingers. "Your highlights are better than hers?"

The last garnered her a soft laugh. Kayleigh reached up and drew the length of her hair over one shoulder, finger-combing it a few times before lifting her ends close to her eyes as if to inspect them. "I don't think she hates me," she said quietly. "At least, I hope not."

"What does your gut tell you?" Emma persisted. "Do you think whoever is posting this stuff is one of your classmates, or someone else?"

Kayleigh dropped her hair, then heaved a heavy sigh, but Emma could see her closing up.

"No clue." She swung her legs over the side of the bed and stood, raising her arms toward the ceiling, then bringing them down in an exaggerated stretch. "I'm tired. I think I'll get ready for bed."

Able to take a hint when it was hurled at her like a javelin,

Emma gathered her computer and the papers. "Cool. I'll be down the hall if you think of anything."

"Okay." Kayleigh strolled into the attached bath, her back straight. "Before you go, I have something for you."

Emma paused in the midst of shoving her things into her computer bag. "Something for me?"

"It's not big," Kayleigh insisted as she emerged again. "Here," she said, thrusting a clear plastic makeup bag filled to bursting with tiny tubes and itty-bitty pots of creams. When Emma hesitated, she dropped it into the open computer bag. "They're free samples I've collected here and there. You can take them. I've got my thing down," she said with an airy wave of her perfectly manicured hand.

"Thanks," Emma replied, almost certain she'd been insulted, but in the best possible way. "I'll check them out."

"'Night," Kayleigh called as she turned on her heel and headed back into the attached bath.

"'Night," Emma returned. "Door open or closed?" she asked as she stepped into the hall.

"Closed, please," Kayleigh called out, and Emma complied.

Standing in the hall, staring at the closed bedroom door, she picked the conversation apart, looking for any useful bits or pieces. At last, she latched on to one thread she needed to yank, and turned away from the guest room to go in search of her host.

She found Max in the media room, stretched out on one of the theater-style reclining loungers. "Please tell me you have a popcorn popper," she said, peering around the doorframe to take in the massive screen mounted to the wall.

Startled, he fumbled for the button to lower the leg rest, but she waved him off. "Don't get up. I only have a question or two, then I'll get out of your hair for the night."

He ignored her command and pressed the button until he was upright, his bare feet planted on the ground.

"Questions for me?"

"Yes." She swung her bag to the floor, then crossed the room to perch on the edge of one of the other massive chairs.

"Okay, but I am sad to report I do not have a popcorn machine."

"Well, now you have something to shoot for. Can you tell me what happened with Tia Severin's father's business?"

"Tia's... Steve Severin?" He looked genuinely taken aback by the change in topic.

"He had a business you helped underwrite?" she queried.

"Yes, I put together some product-development funding for him." Max shifted to look directly at her. "He's an ideas guy working with a couple of buddies who like to tinker, but none of them had a clue where to go from there. Why do you ask?"

"How did you get involved with the company?"

"The usual way." He frowned. "They needed an infusion of cash. They pitched a good product, I put together a group of investors."

"Did the company fail?"

He blinked. "Fail? Not at all," he said, bewildered by the notion. "Why do you ask?"

"Kayleigh told me Tia isn't going to Brown because her dad suffered some financial setback, so she's staying in-state."

"Oh." Max scowled as he pondered the information. "Well, he didn't lose money on our collaboration. We sold to a corporate client almost two years ago. They paid a premium for it, but it's possible he invested his portion of the deal into something else and it didn't fly."

"Are you still in contact with him?"

Max shrugged. "We're friendly when we see one another, but we were never friends."

"You were predominantly business associates," Emma mused.

"Yes."

"But Kayleigh and Tia are close?" she asked.

"They've run around together a lot the last couple years." A crease formed between his eyebrows. "Why? Do you think Tia is involved with this whole mess?"

Emma shook her head. "I don't know, really. I guess I'm picking at loose threads."

Max's phone rang and they both jumped. He picked it up and peered at the screen. "It's Amy Birch," he informed her as he accepted the call with his thumb. "Hello?"

Emma moved to the edge of the cushion and waved to get his attention. When she motioned for him to let her hear, he complied without a moment of hesitation.

"Max? It's Amy Birch."

He met Emma's eyes before answering. "Yes, I still have you in my contacts. How are you? I heard you were injured."

"I'm okay. They're keeping me overnight for observation. I was wondering if you are in contact with the agent investigating the social-media posts?"

Max glanced over at her. "Yes. Special Agent Parker. She's here actually," he said, moving to the seat beside Emma. "I'll put us on speaker."

He pulled a face as he placed the phone on the armrest between them. Emma stifled the urge to laugh at the sheer awkwardness of their situation. Max Hughes was clearly not a man comfortable with subterfuge.

"Ms. Birch?" Emma prompted. "This is Emma Parker."

"Special Agent Parker, thank you for your help this afternoon."

"It's Emma. And we didn't do much. Agent Dawson and I were only sorry we didn't try to get into the school sooner."

"I asked Agent Dawson to wait until the parking lot was clear," she said tiredly. "I had no idea anyone other than Mr. Johnson was in the building."

Emma and Max exchanged a glance. "When I spoke to the LRPD, they said you didn't see your assailant?"

"No. I was in the lab disconnecting the terminal y'all wanted to switch out. I'd gone under the desk to untangle a cable, and when I crawled out, wham!"

Emma winced and touched the top of her own head. "I'm so sorry."

"Thank you." There was a moment's pause, then Amy spoke softly. "I know I'm probably imagining this, but I could swear I heard him say 'Thank you very much.' Of course, I don't think I was fully conscious."

"A polite assailant," Max said grimly.

Emma inched closer to the phone. "You said *him*. Was the voice you heard male?"

"I may be making it all up," she conceded. "The only thing I recall for certain is waking up to find you, Agent Dawson and a paramedic staring down at me."

"Let's not discount what the subconscious mind absorbs," Emma said bluntly. "Intuition has proved to be one of the most valuable tools I have as an investigator." She pulled out her own phone and began typing notes. "Let's assume the person who assaulted you was male. We know for certain two males were in the building at the time Agent Dawson and I arrived—the custodian, Mr. Johnson, and the soccer coach—"

She paused and Amy helpfully supplied a name. "Jake Green."

"Right, thank you," Emma said. There was an awkward beat, then she prompted, "You wanted to talk to me?"

"Yes, I called because something occurred to me," Amy said hesitantly.

"About your attacker?" Emma asked.

"No, about your hacker," Amy corrected. "He—they, whoever it was—took the computer terminal, and maybe this is the knock on the head talking, but I'm not sure it matters."

Curiosity piqued, Emma leaned in. "Why do you say that?"

"Because I reworked the school's network when I came on board last fall. The connectivity was practically Stone Aged, and security nonexistent. I, uh, may have had a copy of some excellent security software acquired by Syscom at my disposal," she said, pitching her voice low and confessional. "I installed it on the school's network."

Intrigued, Emma shot Max a glance as she leaned closer to the phone. "I take it this software was not something available at our local big-box electronics store?"

"No. It was some of the best security software I'd ever come across," Amy said in a rush. "Syscom acquired it from a small company. The head guy was a programmer and really didn't know much about launching a product. I was on the preacquisition evaluation team, so I had copies on both my work and home systems. It was my job to try to break it."

"I see." Emma cocked her head. "Did you?"

"Yes. But then again, I assume you did, too." She paused before filling in the blanks. "You were able to trace the posts back to the school. When I was there yesterday, I saw your footprints in the system."

Emma dipped her head in acknowledgment. "Did you?"

"What was this software called?"

"SecuraT," Amy said. "Secure with an *A* on the end then a capital *T*."

Max stiffened. When she looked up, Emma found him staring straight at her, goggle-eyed.

She tapped the mute button. "You okay?"

"Tell her we'll come see her first thing tomorrow," he ordered.

Emma narrowed her eyes, prepared to push back, but she saw a flash of panic in his eyes, and it stopped her. "Why?"

"We can't talk about this on the phone," he insisted. "What she did was illegal."

Emma sat back, gnawing on the inside of her cheek. There was something he wasn't saying, but as much as she wanted to turn Max upside down and shake him by the ankles until all the answers spilled out, he was right.

She unmuted the call. "This sounds serious, and you may be onto something." She took a deep breath, then spoke slowly, measuring each word to sound logical and not impulsive. "But visiting hours are over, and we've all had a long day. If you don't mind, I'd like to come by the hospital and talk to you first thing tomorrow morning."

"But—"

"Amy, if we're going to stray into corporate-espionage territory, I'd prefer not to speak about it over the phone," Emma stated flatly.

The woman drew in a sharp breath. "Fine. But can you come early? I don't plan to stay in here one minute longer than the doctors say I have to."

"We'll see you first thing," Emma promised.

She ended the call, then turned to look at the man sitting stone-still in his seat. "Your product-development deal... it wouldn't have involved the sale of some software called SecuraT, would it?"

# Chapter Thirteen

Emma shot Max a now-or-never glare. "What am I missing?"

"SecuraT never made it to market," Max informed her gruffly. "It was sold to Syscom as a capture-and-kill."

Emma stared at him, as if trying to absorb this new information and slot it into place. Then she locked on to the bit she needed to complete the code. "A capture-and-kill? Why?"

"Because it was too good," he said, as if his answer should have been obvious. When she stared back at him, he cracked. "It's a fairly common practice. Larger companies buy out their competition all the time."

Max's fingertips tingled but his limbs felt heavy. His whole body felt so heavy he doubted he could lift himself out of his seat if he tried. Emma stared at him, but he didn't know what else to say.

The photo of Kayleigh he used as the wallpaper on his phone caught his eye. Her smile was so wide-open and free it made his heart squeeze. Would he ever see that smile again? She'd come back from this. They all would. But none of them would be the same. Resentment welled up inside him. Frustrated, he picked up the phone and powered it down.

"Oh. Good call," Emma said, pulling out her own phone and shutting it down.

Max didn't have it in him to tell her he was turning off his phone because he was a coward, not because they needed to be cautious.

Shifting in her chair to face him, she asked, "Do you know much about the software itself?"

He shook his head, the corners of his mouth pulling down with disgust at his own ignorance. "No. I mean, I know what it was for, what it was supposed to do, but the technical stuff?" He slowed his shake. "No."

"You saw it demonstrated?"

"Obviously," he replied, a shade too quickly. Aware he was edging into petulant-teenager territory, he shot her an apologetic wince. "I sat through numerous demos. Steve even installed it on my computer, but it's not like software a person actively uses, right? It runs in the background, and unless it throws up a flag—"

"Wait." Emma reached over and gripped his arm. "You have it?"

Max looked down at her fingers wrapped around his forearm. Her grip was urgent, but her palm was warm and comforting. When was the last time someone comforted him? He closed his eyes for a moment, absorbing her heat.

"Max?"

She gave him a gentle squeeze and it was all he could do to keep from jerking his arm from her grasp.

"Huh?"

"You have SecuraT installed on your computer? Your home computer or one at your office?"

He waved his free hand in the direction of his office. "Both."

Her hand slid down and captured his wrist. She tugged hard as she rose. "Come on. Show me."

To his surprise, she didn't let go. She kept her grip firm on his wrist as she led him from the media room, then stood aside to let him take the lead into his home office. Her fingers unfurled when he reached his desk, and he wanted to snatch back her hand. His heart hammered and his pulse thrummed in his head. They were on the edge of something, but he couldn't say whether he was scared or excited by the prospect.

"Log in," she prompted.

Max bent over the keyboard and tapped the space bar to wake the machine. He almost snickered when she looked away to allow him password privacy. "Couldn't you hack your way in?" he asked as his programs loaded.

"I could, but I'm told it isn't nice," she answered, offering him a mockingly prim smile.

Max gave a weak laugh, then stepped back, gesturing for her to take over.

She grabbed the edge of his leather desk chair and pulled the seat close. "You don't keep much on your desktop," she commented as she swirled the cursor around the screen.

"I'm a minimalist."

"I noticed." She chuckled softly as she accessed his operating system. "I'm a mess."

"I noticed," he returned.

She glanced up, shooting him a sidelong glance, a sly smile curving her lips. "We're opposites. Probably why we work well together." He opened his mouth to ask if she truly thought they made a good team, but she cut him off. "Tell me how the deal with SecuraT went. Start from the beginning. With the investment pitch," she clarified.

"Well, Steve Severin is a computer guy. He has a company here in town, SevTech. They mostly do website creation, general IT troubleshooting and some coding for smaller companies. He and a couple guys on his team had been working on SecuraT in their spare time for a couple years."

"And they came to you looking for money to…?" she asked.

He watched as her fingers flew over the keyboard. For every line of nonsense she input, a paragraph of gibberish appeared on the screen.

"Technically, it was to tie up development and ramp up to

distribution. But in reality, he used it to pay his staff so he could free up more time to work on the program itself."

"Would you do me a favor and grab my laptop?"

Max went back to the media room to retrieve her bag. He carried the bag back to the office and placed it on the edge of his desk. "Here you go."

She barely looked up. Eyes glued to the screen, she typed one-handed as she fumbled to find the opening. "Thanks."

He watched her struggle for thirty seconds more, then yanked the bag open so she could grope unimpeded.

"How did the sale come about?" she asked as she pulled out her notebook.

"Steve came to me about eight months and three quarters of the funding in. He was all excited because he thought they had something really good going. They'd done some beta testing using area schools and small businesses. He hired some subcontractors to try to get into the protected systems and only one was successful. Even then, they couldn't deploy anything damaging."

She looked up with an eyebrow raised. "Who were these subcontractors?"

He shrugged. "I didn't get into the nitty-gritty, but I assume some work for larger tech firms. Sort of like headhunters."

"So he thought he had an ace and wanted to see if he could cash out?"

"Cybersecurity is a crowded field with a lot of big names. Steve knew they'd have an uphill battle trying to make a dent in the retail market, no matter how advanced the product." He angled his head to get a better look at what she was doing. She'd opened her own computer and was typing line after line of code into the prompt box. "Are you trying to get into my computer?"

"Testing," she mumbled distractedly. "How'd Syscom get involved?"

"I know the CFO. I knew they had a number of security programs out there, so I told them what we had and a meeting was scheduled."

"How long did it take to get the deal done?" she asked without looking away from her task.

"It was fast. We gave them a window of exclusivity, they did some testing, we had a preemptory offer, acceptance and a done deal within six months."

"Is the timeline unusual?"

"Most don't move so fast, but it's not unheard of," he conceded.

She met his gaze. "I assume you and everyone involved with the sale turned a nice profit?"

He shifted his weight, feeling oddly uncomfortable under her scrutinizing stare. "We're not a bunch of philanthropists, if that's what you're asking," he returned evenly.

She nodded as if his nonanswer told her everything she needed to know. "Twenty bucks says I can break into this thing before we meet up with Amy Birch tomorrow morning."

Narrowing his eyes, he held her challenging stare. "Twenty bucks?"

"Yep."

"You're on." He offered his hand to her, and they shook on the bet.

She ducked her head and began typing again, but Max was fairly sure he heard her mutter "Sucker" under her breath as she dove in.

MAX WAS TWENTY dollars poorer when they arrived at University Hospital the following morning. A plainclothes police officer greeted them at the door to Amy Birch's room.

"Are you here to see Ms. Birch?" he asked, flashing them his Little Rock Police Department detective shield.

They returned his nod of acknowledgment as Emma pulled

her credentials out of her cavernous bag. "Yes. I'm Special Agent Emma Parker with the ASP Cyber Crime Division."

"Nolan Hutchinson," he replied, giving her a not-so-subtle once-over before squinting to inspect her identification.

Emma pretended not to notice, so Max bit the inside of his cheek. No doubt she dealt with guys like Hutchinson all the time. He was smart enough to know any intervention on her behalf would not be welcomed by either party.

"Anything new to report?" she asked.

"I didn't realize the state police had an interest in assault cases," he said, his voice deceptively laconic. He closed the leather wallet and offered it back to her pinned between his index and middle fingers like a playing card.

"We have an open cybercrime case Ms. Birch is helping us unravel," Emma said as she took back the wallet containing her identification.

"I see." He shook his head, his hands planted on his hips and his stance wide and defensive. "No, nothing to report yet. The crime-scene team has been over the computer lab, but they haven't had a chance to process much yet." He glanced back at the closed door. "I spoke with the victim again this morning, but there really isn't much more to add to her story than what we already had."

Max opened his mouth, about to ask whether she had updated the police on her suspicions about her assailant being male, but Emma gave the side of his shoe a kick and he clamped it shut again.

"What kind of cybersecurity issue are you having?" the detective asked.

"A hacker," Emma said in a deliberately offhand manner.

Her clear reluctance to share information with the local police concerning the case frustrated Max as a father, but since he'd been the one to go to the state police rather than the

LRPD, he wasn't about to question Emma's motives in front of this other police officer.

"The school's been hacked?"

Emma nodded. "A school and a number of members of the Capitol Academy community."

Detective Hutchinson hiked up his pants and gave another nod. "I'll leave all the computer stuff to your team," he said as if he was granting them a favor. He pulled a business card out of his pocket and handed it over to Emma. "If you need more information, feel free to reach out to me directly, Special Agent Parker."

"I'll be sure to call if I need your help," she replied, graceful and noncommittal.

The detective brushed past them, and Max turned to watch him saunter down the hall.

"Jerk," Emma said under her breath.

"Yes, he is." Max turned back to her.

The mulish expression on her face told him that he'd chosen correctly on holding his tongue. Convinced the best course of action would be to let her set the tone for the day, he hung back again.

"I want to wait until he's gone before we go in," Emma said in an undertone.

"Not a problem." He leaned up against the wall outside of the hospital room and adopted a casual pose. "So what do you plan to do with your winnings? Aside from gloat over them?"

"Oh, I haven't begun to gloat yet," she answered easily, keeping one eye on the man standing at the elevator banks.

"What do you call the dance you did in the kitchen this morning?"

"Acknowledging my victory," she answered without missing a beat. "Believe me, you'll recognize the gloating when you hear it."

The ding signaling the elevator's arrival echoed down the tiled corridor. "I'll brace myself."

They both turned and watched as Hutchinson stepped into the car. When the elevator doors slid shut behind Hutchinson, Max gestured to the door.

"Shall we?"

"Yep," she replied pertly, pushing into the hospital room. She called out cautiously, "Knock, knock?"

"Come on in," a grumpy female answered in a hoarse voice.

Emma poked her head around the curtain partition. "You said to come early."

"I did," Amy replied, pushing herself up on the bed. "Come on in. It's been a veritable parade in here all night."

"I see LRPD beat me here this morning," Emma commented as she pushed the curtain back.

Max offered a sheepish wave from where he stood. It felt weird, barging into a stranger's hospital room. But Emma didn't seem fazed at all. "Good morning," he said, inclining his head in a greeting.

"Morning," Amy said briefly. "The good part remains to be seen."

Emma drew up a chair and sat down beside the bed. "How are you feeling?"

"Like I've been on a bender for three or four days," Amy replied. "Or at least, how I imagine it would feel. I've never actually been on a bender."

"So, Detective Hutchinson..." Emma said leadingly.

"Is a real jerk?" Amy responded, closing her eyes.

"Exactly."

"Would you mind turning off the overhead lights?" she asked, waving a hand over her head. A strip of obnoxiously bright fluorescent light glared down at them. "I didn't get much sleep and my head is still pounding."

"I'll get it." Max shuffled behind Emma's chair and hit the

switch. Suddenly, the room was lit only by the glow of the light spilling from the attached bathroom. "Better?"

"Loads."

"Are you sure you feel up to doing this now?" Emma asked.

"I don't think there's a lot of time to lose. I was scrolling last night, and there's some pretty ugly stuff being said. The kids are turning on each other. I think the sooner we nip this in the bud, the better."

"Agreed." Emma scooted the chair closer to the bed and lowered her voice. "I was able to get into, uh, the program you mentioned last night."

Amy's eyes flew open. "You were? How?"

"This guy." She hooked a thumb at Max and he rolled his eyes. "Guess whose venture-capital company backed SecuraT's development."

Amy looked up at him, then closed her eyes again and let out a long soft exhalation of disgust. "Of course, you did." She moved her head from side to side on the pillow. "I realize Little Rock isn't a big city, but I never found a more intertwined corner of it than I have at Capitol Academy," she said tiredly.

"It's a fairly insular world," Max agreed. "Steve Severin of SevTech was the developer. You probably had his daughter in your class."

Amy grimaced. Cracking a single eyelid, she gave him a baleful stare. "Severin? Tia Severin?"

Max nodded. "The one and only."

"Of course, it is," she said without rancor. She blinked both eyes open and turned her attention to Emma. "What were the odds of me falling into this job."

Emma chuckled. "Probably pretty good, given your skill set and the caliber of instructor CA employs."

"Flattery will get you everywhere at the moment."

"And let me ask you this," Emma said, wearing the same sly smile from when she'd walked into his kitchen and demanded her twenty dollars. "Were you the only member of the Syscom team who was able to get through the firewalls and breach SecuraT?"

Amy closed her eyes again and simply smiled.

"I think I know what you mean about the coding," Emma told her. "Clever."

"The redundancies threw me at first," Amy said flatly. "I couldn't figure out why they bothered with them."

Max leaned down to Emma. "Some plain talk for the non-tech crowd, please?"

Emma looked up at him. "Even when someone is able to get into the network, it latches on to anyone without the correct access code. Unless they know to break the loop, it literally is like being caught in a trap."

"But whoever was doing this was able to post to various sites using the school's network," he pointed out.

"Yes. And they think they swept their footprints but they didn't," Amy explained with the patience of a natural-born teacher. "Most hackers are really good at covering their tracks, but SecuraT had some interesting scripts written into it. Keystrokes were wiped but not permanently."

Emma nodded eagerly. "They reappear again after a period of time. Kind of like writing a message in invisible ink." Her voice rose with excitement as she warmed to her subject. "Anytime the software detects any kind of attempt to do a data sweep, it captures the original and archives a snapshot. Then it will make it look like it's erasing the data, but it's not. Think of it like making footprints in the sand and wiping them away so no one can follow you."

"Only to have them captured on a map stored in a file cabinet," Amy added. "This is what made the program so valuable." Then she frowned. "Also, what marked it for death."

Max nodded as grim understanding settled in. "A company

like Syscom can't sell security software built to eliminate the need for future purchase of additional security software."

"Right. Letting something like SecuraT loose on the market would have been akin to planning their own obsolescence." Amy sighed. "Software companies may only be as good as their last release, but cybersecurity relies on there being bad actors in the world constantly trying to get past it. Otherwise, no one would be scared enough to invest in it."

"And there are tons of bad guys out there. The state has been the victim of three major malware attacks in the last eighteen months," Emma informed them. "You might have heard a little about them on the news, but trust me, they were way worse than reported."

"Then there was the insurance company whose accounting system was held hostage," Amy added.

Max nodded and crossed his arms over his chest. "It seems like I'm getting a data-breach letter from one financial institution or another every week."

"They've become so commonplace people hardly pay attention to it anymore," Emma said tiredly. "Doesn't mean there isn't major damage being done."

"Exactly," Amy concurred. "SecuraT would have been a great answer for more everyday users, but it also could have been a great jumping-off point for software able to handle the larger clients."

"Were you able to trace whoever is doing these posts in the network?" Max asked, anxious to pull them back on topic. Both women looked up at him, blinking owlishly. As if he'd asked the most ridiculous question a person could conjure. "What?"

Emma took pity on him first. "No. I couldn't find any trace of the posts," she said, her voice unnervingly gentle. She turned to Amy. "Did you?"

The other woman started to shake her head, then stopped on a wince of pain. "No."

Unable to contain his frustration, Max threw up his arms. "Then what's the big deal? Why are you guys so excited, and what are you planning to do to stop this creep?" he demanded, firing his questions at Emma.

She recoiled at first, then sat up. He waited for her to blast him back, but instead, she spoke quietly and calmly. "The big deal isn't what we found, it's what we didn't find." She waited a beat. "Whoever is doing this is someone who has legitimate access to the school's network."

Max started rambling. "So we're back to every student, every teacher, all the adminis—"

"No." The single word spoken by the woman in the hospital bed stopped him mid-rant.

"No?"

"I told you I reworked all the security last fall, remember? The students, teachers and staff all have user access to the network. We could see their activity easily if it were them. We're looking at the people who have administrative access to the network."

"How many people have administrative access?"

"Only three. I sent them an encrypted email with their credentials the day I finished setting it all up."

"Who are they?"

Amy Birch held up three fingers. "Me," she said, lowering one finger. "Dr. Blanton," she said, curling the next one in. "And the president of the school board," she said, lowering the last finger and looking Max straight in the eye.

Emma must have picked up on the undercurrent in what Amy was saying because she shifted in her seat as she divided a look between them. "Who's the president of the school board?" she asked, her tone wary.

Max met her gaze directly. "I am."

He was saved from saying anything more by the attending physician breezing into the room. "Anyone in here ready to go home?"

Emma scrambled to collect her bag and practically jumped up. The chair screeched as it scooted across the tile. Max heard Emma telling Amy to rest and recover, and promising to be in touch soon. But he couldn't make out the teacher's response over the roaring in his ears.

He followed Emma from the room, down the corridor and to the bank of elevators, his mind racing.

"What does this mean?" he asked, slightly out of breath.

Emma raised a hand to halt any further questions. "Let's wait until we're out of here."

He agreed, though the trip down and through the bustling lobby seemed excruciatingly long. Outside, he regulated his long strides to match hers. Still, Emma said nothing. She kept her gaze pointed at the parking deck where they'd left his car. Her jaw was tense. Everything about her manner felt slightly too self-contained, which made him feel like something he couldn't quite grasp was unraveling.

The moment they were in the car, he turned to look at her, his patience worn through. "Okay, we're out. Now, speak to me in short simple sentences."

"Turn your phone off," she ordered, pressing the button to switch off her own.

She waited until he complied, then started in. "Only three people could be behind all this. One of them is the woman lying in a hospital bed, one is in charge of a prestigious school and the other is sitting next to me."

Her hard stare made his breath tangle in his chest. "You think I—"

His indignant protest was strangled by a lack of oxygen. Emma didn't blink. She kept inspecting him with wide hazel eyes. It was the same expression she wore while reading and absorbing line after line of code or data. The gaze of a woman who was accustomed to staring straight at a puzzle until the pieces showed her what they were.

But he was everything he presented himself to be. A man whose life was being turned on its head. "You think I set my child up to be expelled from school weeks before graduation?"

She waited a beat too long before answering. "No."

"You've spent the last few nights sleeping under my roof. Eating meals with me and Kayleigh. Tearing our electronics apart, telling us what we can do and where we can go—"

"Now, wait a minute—" she interrupted.

"No, you wait a minute," he snapped, turning his furious stare on her. "Are you serious?"

She shook her head. "No." She cleared her throat, then spoke louder. "No, I don't think it is you."

"But you thought about it," he challenged.

"Of course, I thought about it," she retorted. "If I didn't consider every possibility, you'd be jumping down my throat for not thinking about it."

He gripped the steering wheel. "It isn't me," he said through clenched teeth.

"And you're absolutely certain there's no way Kayleigh could have intercepted the encrypted email?"

He blew out a breath. "I can't be absolutely sure, no, but come on. What does she have to gain here?"

"I have no idea."

He started the car and shifted into Reverse. "I don't know how much you know about teenagers, but I can promise you there's nothing my daughter is less interested in than my business. Why would she be checking my email?"

Emma propped her elbow on the door and dropped her head into her hand. "You're right. I know nothing about raising a child, but I know teenage girls can be shockingly resourceful when they want to be."

He braked too hard, then shifted the car into Drive. "It's not Kayleigh."

She remained silent. He could practically feel the waves of skepticism wafting off her, and he resented every one of them. He'd trusted her. They'd invited her into their home. Their lives. And now she thought—

"Barricade," she barked in warning.

He stopped inches shy of the exit gate with an angry screech of rubber on asphalt. Heat crept up his neck as he lowered the window. He waved his phone at the scanner and a second later it dinged to signal the acceptance of his payment. When the bar rose, he chanced a glance at her.

"It's not us," he told her flatly as they rolled forward.

"Okay," she said quietly.

"Okay?" He turned to her, stupefied by her abrupt acceptance of his word.

"Okay," she repeated. "I guess I need to do some digging on Dr. Blanton then, don't I?"

# *Chapter Fourteen*

Emma had a shockingly easy time digging up dirt on Samuel Blanton. For a man who went to extraordinary lengths to cover up the trouble he was stirring among the Capitol Academy senior class, he was fairly lax when it came to guarding his own information. But maybe he did that on purpose.

Within an hour of their meeting with Amy Birch, Emma accessed the principal's personal email and from there hacked her way through his financial accounts. Though he made a decent living, the man was by no means well off.

Drumming her pen on the tabletop, Emma wondered if the disparity stuck in his craw. There had to be some children at his school with trust funds worth more than the wealth he'd accumulated over a lifetime.

She found a brokerage account with one of the state's larger firms. She was surprised by some of the transactions she found there. For a man closing in on retirement age, he played fast and loose with his finances.

Drilling down in the data, she found several large investments in emerging tech stocks, including a large buy of shares in Syscom almost three years ago.

She didn't need to look up to know Max was nearby. She could feel the tension vibrating off the man. "When would the sale of SecuraT to Syscom have first been on the table?"

He was by her side within seconds. "The vetting process would have started about three or four years ago. Why?"

"Who else would have known about this potential sale?"

"What do you mean 'who else'?" he asked, frowning.

"You weren't the only investor, right?"

"Right."

"So you and how many other angel investors?" she queried.

"There were six total to start, but only three took an active interest in the product development, aside from myself."

"So four of the six were paying attention?" she asked, clicking around on her screen.

"Yes."

"And the other two were happy to throw money into the pot hoping it paid off?" She failed at masking the edge of disdain in her statement.

"It's not unusual for investors to put money into something and then look away until it's time to cash out."

She hummed her disapproval. "Rich people."

"Why do you ask?" He moved to peer over her shoulder at the screen. "Did you find something?"

"Looks like Dr. Blanton invested heavily in Syscom stock weeks before the sale was finalized. Could be coincidence," she said in a skeptical tone. "Could it be he received a tip?"

"I can't say for certain, but I can tell you Steve Severin wasn't exactly playing it cool when word of Syscom's interest in his product became apparent."

"Do you think it's possible Samuel Blanton caught wind of this potential sale and invested in Syscom believing he was buying in to a company with a surefire hit?"

"Sure, it's possible," he conceded.

"Some people go to jail for buying and selling stock based on confidential information," she said, arching an eyebrow at him.

"Some people do," he said without taking offense. "But in reality, most of them don't."

Emma pulled a notebook close to her and picked up a pen. "Were you able to find some of his employment information?"

"I've got everything," he said flatly.

"Hit me."

"Started at CA about seven years ago. Kayleigh would have been in the lower school grades at the time. I remember him coming in, but I wasn't involved with the school board then."

"What's the general consensus about him among the parents?"

Max shrugged. "He's well-liked. A no-nonsense kind of a guy. A bit on the uptight side, but you want a principal who comes across a bit stodgy, right?"

"I suppose so. If you're a parent," she added with a smirk.

"The school board was doing the hiring, and it's made up of a bunch of parents."

"Okay, so we have a large investment in a tech stock. There hasn't been a huge loss, but also no appreciable return."

"Right now, he's stuck with it because the company has had a rocky patch and he'd lose money if he sold."

"Judging by the numbers, I'm guessing this had to be the bulk of his money. Retirement savings?" she asked, speculating.

"Most likely. But it's about to get worse," Max said darkly. "Rumor has it Syscom will be moving most of their operations overseas in the next two years. Their stock will take a hit the moment it's announced. They haven't brought anything groundbreaking to market in recent years and it could spell disaster for the whole company."

Genuinely perplexed, she asked, "Why wouldn't they pull SecuraT out of their hat and use it to save themselves?"

"There is no SecuraT anymore. They sold it for parts." He held her stunned gaze. "A lot of companies do the same with competing products. They keep what they want to use, bury some bits of it and sell off others."

Emma fixed him with a baleful stare. "I don't mind telling you hearing this hurts my heart."

"Understood." He moved to the chair beside his desk and dropped into the seat. Steepling his fingers, he asked, "So maybe Blanton is seeking revenge on the fathers he feels misled him?"

She fell back into her seat with a sigh. "It's a stretch."

"Sometimes the most implausible ideas have the most potential," he said, tossing off this bit of wisdom with a nonchalant shrug. "Possibility. It's the reason people keep trying."

She blinked at him, then shook her head. "Possibility may fly in the world of venture capital, but when it comes to convincing a judge you need a search warrant? Not so much."

"We have his financials." He pointed to her laptop as if it was the magic bullet.

"We can't use any of this." She actually laughed at his naivete. "I hacked the guy, Max. We need something clean." She sat back and dragged a hand over her face, then glared at her silent cell phone. "We need to prove Blanton was the one to take the computer from the school."

She'd given Simon Taylor the contact information for Detective Hutchinson at the LRPD. The local police had taken all of the school's security footage into custody as part of their assault investigation, but so far, they'd had no word on whether the footage had actually been reviewed yet. Emma knew all too well the department was underfunded and overworked. She could only pray they'd get to checking it sometime soon.

She glanced over at Max, who sat scrolling on his phone. At this point, she wasn't above tapping into any influence he could bring to the table. "Hey, you don't have any contacts with the Little Rock police, do you?"

Max shook his head. "No, but I know the mayor," he said distractedly.

A moment later, she watched his whole face transform as

a smile lifted the corners of his mouth and crinkled his eyes. He held up the phone to show her a contact page with a phone number for the city's highest elected official.

She gestured impatiently for him to get on with it. "What are you waiting for? Make the call."

He chuckled as he did as she asked. He also stood and left the room as soon as the call connected, leaving her to stew as they spoke bigwig-to-bigwig. When he returned less than two minutes later, he gave her a brief nod. "Sorry. I didn't want you to have to listen to me grovel."

She chortled. "Did you?"

He shook his head and dropped back into the guest chair again. "Not really, but let's assume a healthy campaign donation will be expected when the next election cycle rolls around."

"How the sausage is made," she said dryly.

"And how the West was won."

They lapsed into silence as she took another look at the information she'd obtained through what her fellow CCD agents referred to as her special skill set. Max continued to fiddle with his phone as she skimmed the information. She couldn't help wondering who was next on his call sheet. The governor? The FBI?

"What do you think about me giving Steve Severin a call?" he asked, breaking the taut silence.

Emma looked up. "To what end?"

He shrugged. "See if maybe Blanton said something to him about the Syscom investment?"

She pondered the suggestion for a moment, then shook her head. "I think we need to keep things close for now. If we can find something connecting him to the assault, then we'll cast a wider net."

Max hummed, but didn't look up from his phone. "I knew a guy in school who went to work for the FBI," he said a few minutes later. "Simon knows him, too. Never would have picked him to be a Fed," he added with an amused chortle. "He wasn't the straightest arrow in college."

"Most of us weren't," she said, mindful of her own checkered past.

He huffed and dropped his phone into his lap, hauling himself up straighter in the chair. "I can't believe we're stuck here waiting on Hutchinson to do his—"

Her phone lit up. It was a local number without a contact assigned. She eyed it with suspicion before dragging her finger across the screen. "Parker," she said by way of greeting.

"Someone has friends in high places." The caller was a man. She might have had trouble placing him if it wasn't for the insolent edge in his tone.

"Detective Hutchinson," she said, shooting Max a look as she placed the call on speaker. "You're on speaker. Have you found anything useful for us?"

"As I told your boss and the guy you sicced on me from the mayor's office, the timing on the video checks out with Dr. Blanton's alibi. He left the school at four thirty-eight. He was seen at the Johnny Wilkins Steakhouse before the five-thirty meeting began."

Emma and Max shared a glance, then she grasped at her last straw. "Was he carrying anything when he left the school?"

"Briefcase and raincoat," he reported tiredly.

"And everything looked normal? Not bulging or anything?" she persisted.

Her question was met with an exasperated sigh. "I don't know. I guess so. Listen, I'm sorry the lady got knocked on the head, but we see worse—"

She cut him off before he could give her a comparative crime lecture. "I know you're busy. But would you mind sending the file with the video to me? Let us do the poking around."

"You know what? Fine. Knock yourself out," he said gruffly.

Emma didn't waste a moment. "I've got your card here. I'm sending you an email. If you would attach the file and flip it right back to me, I'd appreciate it."

"Yeah. Sure. Okay," he grumbled. "I have a dozen other things I could be doin'—"

"I know. Let me take this off your plate," Emma said solicitously as she hit Send.

"One of the desk jockeys downstairs chopped the file down to the hour before and after the incident," he informed her.

"Perfect." Emma sat back, trying to stifle the urge to grin. Or fist pump. All in all, she thought her restraint was admirable. "If I come up with anything, you'll be the first to know."

"Whatever," Hutchinson responded, then three beeps indicated the call had ended.

"He is quite the charmer," Emma said wryly.

Max flashed a full smile at her. "You'd think he'd watch himself, considering your connections."

Those enticing laugh lines fanning from his eyes melted into devastating dimples, and she almost forgot she was waiting on possible video evidence of a person who'd committed a vicious assault. She was saved from complete oblivion by the chime of her email alert.

She cleared her throat and scooted to the edge of Max's leather executive chair. He stood and came around behind her, bracing his hands on the backrest and leaning in close enough for her to catch a whiff of aftershave. The guy even smelled out of her league.

Keeping her eyes glued to the screen, she clicked the attachment and waited for the video to download.

The split-screen video image showed the interior of the school lobby as well as a wide-angle shot of the steps where she and Wyatt Dawson stood pounding on those impressive carved wooden doors.

"Did they swipe those doors from some medieval castle in Europe or something?" she asked as they watched students and teachers who, she assumed, stayed behind for various activities leave the building, some in chattering groups, others bustling out as fast as they could.

"Actually, they were carved by a group of artisans up near Mountain Home. Took them three years to complete each one, and if you look closely, you notice they share a motif, but they're all unique."

"Huh. Like snowflakes," she said distractedly. A slender dark-haired girl she recognized from Kayleigh's social-media accounts rushed through the lobby and hit the crash bar on the center door at full speed. "Whoa, someone's in a hurry," she said under her breath.

"Tia Severin," Max explained.

Emma looked up at him, shocked to have captured one of the minor players in this drama in action. "That was Tia?"

Max nodded, then pointed to the screen. "Freeze it."

She hit the space bar and the playback stopped.

He pressed his finger to the side of the monitor with the outdoor scene. At the edge of the shot, she saw an oversize luxury SUV with pricey guards over the taillights.

"That's Steve Severin's truck. He must have been picking Tia up," he said, then leaned back.

Emma gaped up at him in disbelief. "Are you telling me they were both there—" she checked the timestamp on the playback "—ten minutes or so before Amy Birch ends up getting clocked with a computer?"

Max pulled a face, his lips now flattened into a grim line. "Not as much of a coincidence as you'd like to think it is. Tia wrecked her car last month. She'd been riding to and from school with Kayleigh every day until…"

He let the rest go unspoken, but Emma could not resist filling in the blanks. "Until Kayleigh was suspended." She restarted the playback and they lapsed into silence, the tension in the room sickening as the timestamp inched closer to 4:38 p.m.

"What if…" Max began and then stopped. "There he is."

Emma hit the button to pause the playback as he spoke. They leaned in. Dr. Blanton carried a briefcase made of black leather in one hand and had his raincoat draped over the opposite arm. He was in the process of pushing against the door, his hip pressing the bar to release the latch.

"Play it through," Max whispered.

She unpaused the video, and they watched the principal bustle through the door into the wet afternoon, his head bent and his steps quick.

The misty rain blurred the view picked up by the wide-angle camera. Emma cocked her head and peered at the footage intensely as the older man descended the steps, his head down.

"Why isn't he wearing the coat?" she asked aloud.

Beside her, Max hummed. "It wasn't raining hard."

"True, but he has it," she argued, backing the playback up to the lobby and letting it run again. They watched his departure play through without interruption. The second the man disappeared from the frame, she skipped back again. "I had my windbreaker on. So did Wyatt," she murmured as she reset the video. "Why wouldn't he put the coat on?"

"Too warm?" Max said, hazarding a guess.

She paused the video again at the spot where he pushed against the heavy door. With a few keystrokes, she isolated the hand holding the briefcase. "Is it in there?" she murmured, trying to enhance the image enough to see if it bulged.

"Nah, wouldn't fit," Max said confidently.

She looked over her shoulder at him. "How do you know?"

"Because I have one exactly like it. It's a Karl Legstrom Palladium bag," he explained, rattling off the name.

When he saw the information meant nothing to her, he moved to the opposite side of the desk and picked up a slender leather satchel in a rich forest-green. It was identical to the one Dr. Blanton carried in every way except color.

"You can fit a laptop and maybe a few files in here, but not a desktop unit."

"They were small units," she countered, though she had to admit the CPU would have been too blocky to fit in the slim briefcase.

"Maybe he's carrying it out," Max suggested.

She backed out of the close-up and switched to the opposite arm. "Might explain why he didn't put the coat on," she grumbled.

"Why is it bothering you?" he asked, his tone amused.

"Because it does," she said with a shrug. Then she zoomed in on the coat draped over the crook of his arm and her breath caught. "Or maybe I knew all along?" she said, slowly turning to look at Max. "Do you see what I see?"

Max nodded. "Chalk one up for the lady."

She screen-captured the image and used some of the editing tools to draw red circles around the areas of interest. "I'm not a lady, I'm a cop," she mumbled as she worked.

"Or maybe you're both," he challenged.

She snorted but said nothing more as she fired off an email to Simon Taylor, attaching both the security video and the screen captures.

"Do you think it'll be enough?" Max asked as she hit the button to send the email.

"For a search warrant? It should be." She turned and looked at him full-on. "For an arrest? There are still a lot of dots to connect."

"You'll connect them."

He sounded so certain she couldn't work up enough false modesty to deny him. She would. Not only because it was the

job, but also because these people—Kayleigh, Max and even
Amy—had let her in on a personal level. They believed in her.
They let her in. There was no way she was going to let some
bitter old guy with an overdeveloped sense of entitlement and
a misplaced grudge hurt them any more than he already had.

Reaching over, she covered Max's hand and squeezed. "I
will. I'll connect every last one of them."


EMMA RANG DR. BLANTON'S doorbell that afternoon with Simon
Taylor standing by her side, as silent and self-contained as ever.

A team of agents who specialized in the systematic search
for evidence gathered behind them, unloading evidence boxes
and donning the gear designed to keep their DNA from con-
taminating anything seized. They had a few members from
the LRPD evidence-recovery team mixed in with the group,
but when he heard about the issuance of the warrant, Detective Hutchinson was more than happy to let the state do the
nitty-gritty work.

"What?" Samuel Blanton blustered when he opened his
door to find a small law-enforcement army assembled on his
porch. "What's the meaning of this?"

"Special Agent Emma Parker and Special Agent in Charge
Simon Taylor, sir," she stated formally. "We have a warrant to
search these premises."

"A warrant," he repeated, face reddening with outrage.
"Whatever for?"

"Sir, we believe you may have evidence connected to the
assault on one of the Capitol Academy teaching staff as well
as the ongoing cyberbullying and stalking of a minor student."

"This is…"

He sputtered then stopped when Simon unfolded the warrant and thrust it at the man.

"You're welcome to contact your attorney," Emma informed
him, "but the search will begin now."

She and Simon stood beside Dr. Blanton, search warrant in hand as the team marched into the midcentury home far from the school. Wyatt was watching over another team as they swept the man's office at Capitol Academy. Max was with him, overseeing the search as a representative of the school board. The warrant also covered searching Dr. Blanton's vehicle, but they'd all agreed the home and office took precedence.

Blanton pulled his phone from his pocket and began furiously scrolling through his contacts. Emma waved the warrant she'd refolded. "I'm sorry, sir," she said as she plucked the phone from his grasp. "I'm afraid I have to confiscate all electronic devices."

"But I need to call my attorney," he protested.

"You're welcome to use a landline, if you have one," she said, not backing down.

"I no longer have a landline," Blanton huffed.

At last, Simon spoke up. "I'll be happy to place the call for you. What's your attorney's name?"

Emma deftly bagged the man's phone, then handed it to Simon, leaving the subject of their investigation to her boss to handle. Turning to the two officers in full hazmat gear still standing on the steps, she gave them a wan smile.

"Are you my raccoons?" she asked, using the term they jokingly used for the officers assigned to going through a suspect's trash.

"Yes, ma'am," the one on the right answered.

"Better sweep the yard before it gets dark. Pick up everything. We know our assailant shattered the plastic casing on the computer, so pick up every tiny bit of whatever you find not created by Mother Nature. I'm talking old gum wrappers. Got me?"

"Yes, ma'am," they answered in unison, then took off around the side of the house.

TWO HOURS LATER, Emma was at her desk at state police head-quarters, dwarfed by the contents of Samuel Blanton's desk drawers. Two banker boxes filled with tax returns and other financial documents sat at her feet. "Everything posted from the cloned socials in the last two days came from a mobile device," Caitlin called over the partition.

"An excellent place to start," Emma called back.

When Emma arrived at headquarters with her bounty, she'd asked Caitlin Ross to move to one of the empty desks closer to the cubicle she shared with Wyatt Dawson so they could talk as they worked.

Wyatt had dropped everything they'd found at the school on her desk and then taken off with Simon Taylor with a rushed apology. They'd been called to a meeting at the local offices of the Bureau of Alcohol, Tobacco, Firearms and Explosives in connection with a case they were working with the ATF as part of a joint task force.

Which left Emma and Caitlin to go through all the evidence they'd amassed in the search-and-seizure. Starting with the electronics seemed only logical to them both. Emma had Blanton's mobile and tablet, while Caitlin had his laptop, desktop from the academy and a box full of external hard drives, flash drives and outdated mobile phones.

Emma focused on the phone in her hand. Cords and cables snaked across the surface of her desk. She glanced over her shoulder, then back to her own phone, which remained mad-deningly silent. She hadn't heard from Max after the search of the school office was complete. She didn't know why she expected to, but she did. And now here she was, alone again—

"Since they ditched us with all the work, we should order pizza. Or maybe Thai," Caitlin called over the wall.

Emma smiled. She wasn't alone. She was hungry and tired, that was all. "Pizza would be easier."

"What's your favorite place?" Caitlin called over the up-holstered wall. "Do you eat meat?"

She'd just typed the command to run a diagnostic test on Blanton's mobile when a familiar voice cut off her answer.

"Emma?"

She frowned, planting her hands on her desk as she rose to peek around the corner of the partition. "Max?"

"Where are you?" he called above the warren of cubicles.

Part of her didn't want to answer. She'd spent hours working out of his beautifully appointed home office. The last thing she wanted was for him to see the shabby seventeenth-hand desk where she toiled like Cinderella, day in and day out.

"Emma?" he called again. "I brought dinner."

She sighed and stepped out into the narrow corridor. Caitlin rolled out her desk chair. "Who's there? He sounds cute."

Emma shot the younger agent a scornful glance. "How can someone sound cute?"

Unperturbed, Caitlin shrugged as Emma passed. "I don't know. He does."

Poking her head around the end of the set of cubicles, Emma caught sight of the man in question. He *was* cute. Or more than cute. He was Prince Charming handsome. The thought brought her right down to earth again. She was a woman who had both shoes snugly on her feet.

"We're over here," she called, waving an arm.

His face lit with a smile as he caught sight of her, and her traitorous heart did a flip. "Hey. I thought you might be hungry," he said, holding up a large carryout bag.

She was about to wave him off, but then her stomach growled loudly, blowing what cover she had left. "We are," she conceded.

"It's only subs," he said with a shrug. "I wasn't sure how many people you'd have around so I ordered a variety box." He handed over the bulging bag.

"Thank you." She heard the rumble of chair casters on a carpet mat and knew Caitlin had ducked back into the space next to hers. Smiling tiredly, she said, "Come on back. This is the really glamorous part of the job where we get to pretend we're trash pandas."

# Chapter Fifteen

"Trash pandas?" Max asked, torn between bewilderment and bemusement.

"We're like raccoons—we gather everything we can, then dig through all of it."

She gave him a wan smile and he had to tuck his hand in his pocket to keep from brushing her hair back from her cheek.

"Where's Kayleigh?" Emma asked as she placed the carry-out bag on an empty desk.

He frowned and looked around. Surely this couldn't be hers. "She's staying with the Marshes for dinner."

"They had a good day together?"

"Yeah. Kayleigh sounded really happy when I spoke to her."

"Did you tell her what we had going on?"

"Broad strokes," he replied. "I didn't want to bog her down with details when she was finally thinking about something else."

"Good call," Emma concurred. "I'm glad she and Patrice have been able to reconnect. I hope it will be helpful for both of them." She turned and called, "Hey, Ross, you can come out now!"

"Ross?" Max asked. "I thought you worked with that Dawson guy who was at the school."

"Wyatt Dawson and I share space here, but he's out on another assignment." She looked over her shoulder and spotted Caitlin approaching, her steps slow and her eyes wider than usual. "Special Agent Caitlin Ross, this is Max Hughes," she said, waving a hand between them. "He's a compulsive feeder."

Caitlin extended her hand. "My favorite kind of person."

Emma unwrapped a club sandwich, plucked the lettuce and tomato from it and took a voracious bite.

"Help yourself," he said, releasing the woman's hand to gesture to the bag. "I thought I'd come see if I can help."

Emma harrumphed as she chewed, eying his pristine polo shirt and perfectly faded jeans. "I could send you down to sort through the actual trash."

He raised both eyebrows. "You took his trash?"

"You'd be surprised how many people simply throw incriminating evidence in the garbage. People who commit acts of violence aren't always as clever after the fact."

"Unless they're a serial killer," Agent Ross said with a nod, plucking a bag of chips from the bag.

Emma waved the uneaten half of her sandwich as if conceding the point. "Right. Premeditated is a different animal. But most assaults are matters of circumstance."

"Wrong place at the wrong time," Agent Ross agreed, opening the bag of chips.

"You think he tossed the computer he used to hit Amy Birch in his garbage at home," Max said, unable to hide his skepticism.

"Oh. No. He had the computer in the trunk of his car," Emma informed him. She snagged a bag of chips, then gestured for him to follow. "Come with me."

Max grabbed one of the wrapped sandwiches from the box then hustled after her, flashing the other agent a quick smile. "Feel free to share those with whoever is around," he called back.

"Share them?" Caitlin scoffed. "Maybe after I load my mini fridge."

Max's chuckle died on his lips as he rounded a corner and

came to an abrupt halt. Every surface of the two-person cubicle space was covered with piles of paper, files, boxes overflowing with electronics and cords and banker boxes filled with what he could only assume were hard copies of some of the financial records Emma accessed online.

"Holy cow."

"You said you wanted to help," she reminded him, leaning over the desk to check the screen of a mobile phone attached to her computer. "Clean. Damn it," she muttered, dropping into her chair.

"If you have the computer, why are you—"

"We have the remains of the computer," she informed him. "Looks like he ran over it a couple times, then tossed the remains into his trunk." She sighed. "I assume he planned to give it a couple days, then go throw it in a dumpster somewhere."

She unplugged the smartphone and set it atop a stack of files.

"So it's no good as evidence?" He wandered into her space and poked through one of the piles at random. It appeared to contain printouts of several school-board meetings. Max frowned, wondering why Blanton had bothered to print them. His own copies were all filed away in his email archives.

"It's great evidence for the assault charge," she said distractedly. "But we need to find something connecting him to the hacking."

Max pulled up short. "Have the Little Rock police arrested him?"

Emma shook her head. "Not yet. I haven't called Hutchinson yet. His case is pretty open and shut, but we need something more."

"What if Blanton tries to leave?" Max demanded, his voice rising as he envisioned the slimy old creep slipping away.

"He can try," Emma said, looking up at him, her head tilted to the side. "But the agent we have parked in front of his house will stop him." She turned back to her task. "I need some time. If I don't have it by morning, I'll let Hutchinson pick him up and we'll make our case later. But if we find a connection between Blanton and the stalking and harassment, it makes the assault case stronger."

"Piling on the charges," Max murmured. He pulled a leather portfolio he'd seen the principal carrying to board meetings and dropped into the chair behind Emma.

"We call it improving our batting average," she retorted. "Caitlin says the last few posts made to any of the cloned accounts came through mobile applications, so we're trying to locate the device."

He flipped through the lined pages of notes Blanton had jotted during various meetings. His eye was drawn to the name *Michael Pierce* scrawled on the third page. It had been underlined so vigorously Blanton had nearly torn through the paper.

"Hey," he called softly. "Do you remember seeing the name of Blanton's stockbroker anywhere?"

"No, why? I wouldn't take any tips from him if I were you," she said, flipping through apps on the tablet she had connected to her laptop.

"Does the name *Michael Pierce* mean anything to you?"

She shook her head, then raised it slowly. "Michael Pierce? Like Carter Pierce?"

"His father." Max cleared his throat and sat up, skimming the piles of paper around them, hoping to spot a brokerage statement.

"Do you think he's the one Blanton used to buy the Syscom stock?"

"I don't know. I only know his name was written in the margin of this notepad," he said, extending the portfolio for her to see.

Emma swiveled to look. Their knees touched as she leaned

in, but if one of them was going to pull away, it would have to be her. "Wow, written and struck through," she murmured.

"I think he was underlining, but yeah. Fairly emphatic," he concurred.

"Hey, Cait?" Emma called over the wall. "Aside from Kayleigh Hughes, who else do we have confirmed cloned social-media accounts?"

"Um..." There was a shuffle on the other side of the wall. "Kayleigh Hughes and Carter Pierce are confirmed. Tia Severin and Patrice Marsh possibly," she called back.

"Huh," Emma grunted.

Max murmured a soft expletive, which she ignored as she pointed to the banker boxes by her feet.

"Look in one of those. They're the files pulled from his desk at home."

Max bit his lip to stifle his protest when she spun away from him. They were working on something together. Something important. In a way, they were as connected as those kids were. And together, they'd get to the bottom of this. Tonight.

He tossed the portfolio on top of another pile and bent to grab one of the boxes, but he misjudged the stability of the pile. Gravity caught the heavy leather folder and pulled it down with a flutter of loose pages. It hit the floor with a thud and fell open.

"Hey, don't mess things up," Emma chided. "I know it looks like chaos to you, but it's controlled chaos."

Max cursed and abandoned his banker's box, only to freeze when he caught sight of two colorful plastic cards with the logo of a popular pay-as-you-go cellular service emblazoned on the top.

He looked up with a frown, his brain whirring as he tried to slot pieces into place. "Hey, Em?" he called, hoping his thoughts would coalesce before she answered. He needn't have worried because she didn't respond. He swallowed hard and tried again. "Emma?"

"Hmm?" she said, tapping furiously on the tablet.

He squinted at the device she'd already set aside. "What model is Blanton's phone?"

"Huh? Oh. It's the new one. Same as yours and Kayleigh's," she said, waving her hand dismissively. "But it's clean. I checked it already."

"You can get this phone on a pay-as-you-go plan," he murmured, half to himself.

"What?" She half turned, her attention snagged.

He pulled the cards from the inner pocket of the leather binder and handed them to her. "Why would he need these if that's his phone?" He nodded toward the high-end phone.

Emma flipped over the cards. "Someone has peeled off the sticker concealing the activation codes." She raised an eyebrow. "Where were these?"

He held up the portfolio. "Inside pocket."

Tossing the tablet onto her desk, Emma shot out of her seat. "Caitlin? Grab the box with the old phones," she ordered. "I think we're looking for a burner."

THEY HAD TWO PHONES, a smashed computer and more technical information regarding digital footprints of more security breaches than any judge ever wanted to see by the time Simon Taylor returned to headquarters.

Emma met her boss at the door. "We have him," she announced breathlessly. She looked beyond Simon. "Where's Wyatt?"

"I sent him home," he responded. "I didn't know he'd be needed."

Emma nodded, a frown tugging at her mouth. "He's not, really. I have everything we need. I need you to get on the phone with Detective Hutchinson's commanding officer and spell out all the reasons it would be better for them if we took the assault case off their plate."

Simon looked up from the sheaf of papers she'd thrust into his hands. "You giving the orders now, Parker?"

Her cheeks flared, but she swallowed the impulse to apologize for her strident tone. In the end, she settled for a simple reply. "No, sir."

Simon craned his neck to look past her. She didn't need to turn around to know Max had followed her, even though she specifically told him not to.

"What are you doing here?" he asked, his tone clipped.

Emma jumped in before Max could answer. "He's been helping."

Again, with the single eyebrow lift. But Emma felt no compulsion to justify Max Hughes's presence. Simon had been the one to assign her to the case. He told her to stick close. To get as much information as she could out of his old friend and do everything in her power to keep him and his daughter safe. She'd done exactly as instructed.

"He was leaving," she informed her boss. Turning back to Max with a pointed glare, she said, "I'll let you know as soon as we have him in custody."

"But—"

She cut him off with a raised hand. "You need to get home to Kayleigh. We don't want her alone in the house until all this comes out," she reminded him.

Simon stepped up beside her, handing the paperwork she'd so carefully put together for his perusal back without another glance. "She's right. We'll handle things from here."

Max opened his mouth, but then snapped it shut. Max probably knew Simon better than she did, but they both knew there was no point in arguing when he'd decided on a course of action. He locked eyes with her.

"You'll let me know as soon as you have him?" he asked.

Emma softened his dismissal with a smile. "Agent Vance is parked outside his house, remember? We already have him."

"Emma, please," Max said, taking a step closer. "I'll… Kayleigh and I will be worried."

She caught his quick rewording. There was no doubt Simon had, too. And as twisted as it sounded, she had to admit, it felt good knowing someone would be worrying about her.

"I'll call the minute we leave his house."

AGENT VANCE ACCOMPANIED her to the door but hung back as she pressed the bell.

That Simon Taylor hadn't come out to make the arrests with her, nor had he called Wyatt to come back on duty bolstered her confidence.

This was her case.

Her collar.

Negotiations with the LRPD were remarkably smooth. They balked at first, but once they started hitting them with the technical information they had against Samuel Blanton, Emma could practically hear Hutchinson and his lieutenant's eyes rolling back over the phone.

She smiled to herself as she rang the bell a second time. There were advantages to working in a field people preferred not to know too much about.

Samuel Blanton opened the front door. He was still dressed in the clothes he wore earlier in the day.

As a matter of formality, Emma held up her credentials even though the man had inspected them thoroughly earlier, and said, "Samuel Blanton, I'm Special Agent Emma Parker of the Arkansas State Police Cyber Crime Division. You are under arrest."

The older man rolled his shoulders back and tipped his chin up, trying to maintain the dignity he'd sacrificed the minute he cloned Kayleigh Hughes's accounts.

"On what charge?" he demanded.

"Charges," Emma corrected, emphasizing the plural. "We have evidence you assaulted Ms. Amy Birch in the computer lab of Capitol Academy yesterday afternoon."

He opened his mouth to protest, but she held up her hand.

"We also have evidence you created multiple social-media accounts using the likenesses of minor children. We also have evidence of computer hacking, unauthorized surveillance and stalking. All involving one or more minors." She tipped her head to the side. "Shall I go on? There are more, but those are the heavy hitters."

"I'll need my phone to call my attorney," he said stiffly.

Emma inclined her head, making no comment on how ineffective his attorney had been in pushing back against the search warrant.

"You can call him from headquarters," she replied curiously. "Please turn and place your hands on the wall."

"You can't be serious," Blanton said in a tone so deeply offended Emma doubted herself for a moment.

Most people who committed cybercrimes weren't the violent type, but this man had attacked Amy Birch. Was the assault on the teacher a matter of circumstance, or did he have violent tendencies?

"Sir, please place your hands on the wall," she said briskly, stepping into the foyer and pulling on his arm until he faced the wall.

Once his palms were spread flat against the plaster, she nudged his feet apart in preparation for a pat down. But his foot hit the leg of a spindly hall table, sending a stack of mail cascading to the floor and momentarily distracting her. Emma rose from her squat as Blanton spun, snatched a long-handled letter opener from the table and wielded it like a knife.

"Step back," he ordered.

Emma remained in a semicrouch, hands open to show her empty palms.

She heard Vance as he barked, "Freeze!" She didn't have to look back to know he'd drawn his weapon and had it trained on the man in front of her.

"Everyone stay calm," she cautioned, her voice deceptively steady. "Dr. Blanton, threatening me will not get you anywhere. The judge has a record of the evidence we've collected, as do the Little Rock police," she informed him. "You have nothing to gain from harming me, and everything to lose."

"I've already lost everything," he shouted, his voice trembling as violently as his hand. "I have nothing left. Nothing!"

"You have your life," she reminded him. "And I can guarantee you will not if you make a move on me. Agent Vance is an excellent shot. There's one way for you to walk away from here tonight, and it can only happen if you put your weapon down."

The older man seemed to be weighing his options. While he huffed and puffed like an exercised horse, she took the opportunity to straighten up and slid her right foot closer to the left, alleviating the burning sensation in her quads and giving Vance a cleaner shot if necessary.

"You can't possibly connect me to those horrible things those spoiled miscreants say to one another on their webchat programs. I know nothing about internet…waves."

Emma saw the sharp glint of cunning in the man's blue eyes. She didn't for one second believe he was as inept as he wanted her to believe, but if it got him talking, she was willing to play along.

"Well, I suppose it's possible someone is trying to frame you," she said, drawing each word out as if she was giving it consideration. "Someone was pitting the students against one another, and all the digital evidence points to you."

"But digital evidence can be manipulated, can it not? With artificial intelligence and all?"

He waved the letter opener, and Emma leaned back instinctively to evade any incidental contact. If he wanted to start building his defense now, she had no issue. She'd simply keep piling on the evidence. He'd used the access he'd gained through her apps to snake his way into her networked devices and invaded the privacy of a minor in myriad ways. The charges she could lay at his feet went well beyond hacking.

Then she heard a soft "Oof!" behind her, followed by an outraged Vance, who shouted, "Hey, stop!"

Before she or Blanton could react, Max Hughes barreled through the front door and shoved her suspect up against the wall, one hand on the man's throat, the other pinning the wrist of his right hand to the wall.

The letter opener clattered to the floor and Emma planted the sole of her shoe on top of it.

"What do you think you are doing?" she demanded of Max. "Have you lost what sense you were born with?"

"He was pointing a knife at you," he huffed, glaring down at the shorter man.

"It was a letter opener," Emma said through gritted teeth, "and we had it under control."

She stepped aside to give Tom Vance the room to step inside. He'd holstered his weapon and was removing a set of cuffs from his windbreaker pocket.

"Did you think you were going to make some kind of citizen's arrest?"

"I didn't think," Max admitted.

He loosened his grip on the reddening man's throat only slightly when Tom caught Blanton's flailing left arm and clapped the cuff on. Tom chuckled when Max yanked Blanton's hand across the front of his body, presenting the man's right wrist to be cuffed.

"Thank you," the agent said gruffly.

Emma watched as Blanton visibly shrank under Max's unrelenting stare. Tom had to elbow Max out of his way to get to Blanton. But Max kept his gaze locked on the older man until he was led out the door.

"He threatened your life and tried to steal Kayleigh's future," he said, breathless. "I couldn't let him...there's no way I will let him get away with any of this."

"Not your job," she said dryly. Digging her elbow into his side, she waited until he tore his gaze from Blanton and focused on her. "Protecting me is not your job."

"You've been protecting me. And Kayleigh," he added hastily.

"*Literally* my job," she retorted.

He turned to face her, gray eyes boring into hers as his chest rose and fell dramatically. She wanted to press her thumb to his wrist and feel the adrenaline pulsing through his veins, but she resisted.

"I am the one trained to protect and serve," she said quietly.

Max nodded, his Adam's apple bobbing as he swallowed hard. "And you're good at it."

"I didn't need you rushing in here like a maniac. I had it under control," she assured him.

"I know you did."

She scoffed. "And yet, here we are. Do you have any idea how much ribbing I'm—" Words fled her when he slid his hand up to cradle her nape, his fingers tangling in her hair. "What are you—"

"You might have things under control, but I saw him and I..." His gaze dropped to her mouth. "Emma."

"Max," she answered.

"I've wanted to kiss you for days," he confessed.

"What's stopping you?"

And then he was. His mouth was warm and firm. The kiss was commanding, but somehow not overbearing. He angled his head, slanting his mouth across hers for a better fit, and a small groan escaped her. It was every bit as perfect as the man himself.

"What are we doing?" she asked when they broke for air.

"What I've wanted to do since the first time you wandered into my kitchen looking for coffee," he answered gruffly. "You were a mess."

"Still am," she whispered, stretching up on her toes in a blatant invitation.

He took it, kissing her so slowly and softly she barely cared that they were standing in an open doorway spotlit by foyer and porch lights. So tenderly, she would tolerate any amount of torment Vance and the other agents wanted to dish out. This kiss was worth it.

"A beautiful mess," he whispered across her kiss-dampened lips. "Best mess I've ever seen."

\* \* \* \* \*

# **HARLEQUIN**
## Reader Service

# Enjoyed your book?

Try the perfect subscription for Romance readers and g
more great books like this delivered right to your door.

See why over 10+ million readers have tried
Harlequin Reader Service.

## **Start with a Free Welcome Collection with free books and a gift—valued over $20.**

Choose any series in print or ebook.
See website for details and order today:

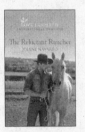
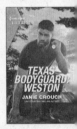

# **TryReaderService.com/subscriptions**

RSBPA